Inked

A Broken Sparrow Novel

AMITY MALCOM

Playlist

Sweet Baby James-James Taylor
Beautiful-Carole King
Cleopatra-The Lumineers
Mud On The Tires-Brad Paisley
Super Bass-Nicki Minaj
Say You'll Be There-Spice Girls
Stay (Wasting Time)-Dave Matthews Band
Beggin'-Maneskin
You Should Probably Leave-Chris Stapleton
Monster-Mumford & Sons
One And Only-Adele
Unsteady- Erich Lee Gravity Remix
-X Ambassadors, Erich Lee
Party In The U.S.A.-Miley Cyrus
Let It Be Me-Ray LaMontagne
You Are My Sunshine-Johnny Cash
Love Like This-Ben Rector
Beyond-Leon Bridges

Dedication

To my other half-

Thank you for always pushing me to achieve my goals.

To my mom-

Please gloss over the sex scenes.

While a work of fiction, Inked lightly touches on the themes of domestic violence and non-consensual sex.

One
MINA

STANDING in the never-ending security line, I can't help but feel nervous. Seven years have passed since I last stepped foot into the small town I grew up in. Johnson Creek wasn't exactly a thriving metropolis; in fact, the three whole stoplights that stretched down Main Street (yes, we had an *actual* Main Street) made it anything but. The town's streets were dotted with long-standing businesses that had been passed down through family, extending generations upon generations. Sure, I wanted to go back more frequently - wanted to be closer with my family than I was, but life got in the way. Doesn't it always have a way of doing that?

A long sigh escapes my lips as I slowly snake my way through the stanchions towards the frowning TSA agents, thinking back to the promise my brother and I made to each other seven years prior. Standing on the front porch after burying our father, we promised each other that while our lives may have gone in dramatically different ways, if we ever needed one another, all we had to do was ask. And last week, he asked.

Colin, six years older than me, has his shit together. He has a successful career as a small-town attorney, two cute kids, an even more adorable dog and – up until three months ago – a beautiful wife that doted on all three of them. He still had our mother who had moved into the beautiful house he shared with his late wife Tabitha and their children, but he said he needed more. Colin was a family man - the golden child growing up. I didn't resent him for that; I wasn't mad that he chose a more traditional career while I followed my artistic endeavors. I wasn't angry that he had settled down, creating a family while I ran from shitty relationship to shitty relationship. We were close growing up despite our age difference, and we remained close, even with me across the country. We even spoke on the phone and through FaceTime calls several times a week.

So here I was, hoping to avoid a full body pat-down and praying the vibrator in my overstuffed carry-on duffle bag didn't set off the x-ray machine. I left my busi-ness - a successful all-female operated tattoo shop in downtown Portland - in the hands of my business partner and best friend Daphne. I bought the first and cheapest ticket I could find and was leaving my life on the west coast behind after a five day whirlwind of teary goodbyes. I wasn't sure how long I was going to be back east, but something in my bones told me it would be longer than the one month we had already planned for.

After a successfully uneventful security check, I grabbed my wheeled carry-on and duffle bag and shuffled towards my gate, eager to get to Johnson Creek. I never felt the pull to my childhood home, but this time- knowing I was truly needed- it felt different. I hated going back under the circumstance of my brother's broken heart, but to my surprise, I wasn't dreading the time I would be spending with my family. Actually, when I reflected on my feelings, I felt a slight bit of excitement in knowing I would soon be surrounded by familiar small-town sights.

After tracking down my gate and finding an available seat in the terminal, I swipe through a few emails that had trickled in, my thumb hovering over one from Broken Sparrow - a tattoo shop and Johnson Creek institution. One of the first legal tattoo shops in North Carolina and in business for much longer than that, it has been operated by the same family for several generations, making it a popular spot for quality guest artists.

People would travel from neighboring, larger cities to see the artists that frequented the shop. Not knowing how long I would be home, I was hoping to pick up a few days each week at the shop when Colin and my mom didn't need help with the kids or sorting through Tabitha's once full life.

Opening the email, I quickly scan the contents and let out an unintentional, audible squeal along with a small shimmy in my chair when I see that Thom, the current owner, wants me to come in to see him and talk about my potential guest spot. Fingers flying over the built-in keyboard of my phone, I let him know that I'd give him a call when I got settled in, hit send on the message and look up to find a man staring at me from the seat across the terminal aisle with a Cheshire cat grin on his face.

"Sounds like good news for you, doll," he almost snorts.

Taken aback, my eyes dart back to my phone while my cheeks flush with heat. His almost abrasive tone takes me aback, yet I can't stop myself from stealing another glance at him over the top of my phone screen when I think he isn't looking my way.

Good looking, sure. Smug...*absolutely.*

He's slouched in the chair, legs spread in an overt display of masculinity while he fingers a copy of Architectural Digest. Fitted jeans cling to his legs while a button-up, beige cardigan, covers a thin, white tee. His hair is short, almost buzzed on the sides while somewhat longer on top. It is slightly graying on the sides and fades to deep browns on top. His deep, brown eyes – much like the color of his hair – are framed by a pair of chunky, dark-framed glasses that are fitting of the typical, Portland hipster style. I can tell he has body art across his chest from the swirling patterns peeking out of the top of the white shirt and I have the sudden desire to trace my fingertips across the designs inked on his tanned olive skin.

From his looks, he appears to be the type of man who isn't frequently told "no". He wears a self-righteous smile and I can tell that his clothing is hiding an impressive display of muscle.

I snap back to my current surroundings when the desk attendant's voice begins the boarding process over the loudspeaker. I notice the God-like stranger let out another low chuckle as he stands and wheels his carry-on towards the door of the breezeway that leads to the plane. He's shaking his head back and forth as if amused with a secret only he knows. A few short minutes later, I do the same- minus the sardonic chuckle- as my boarding group is called.

When it comes my time to step onto the plane, I am

miraculously able to find overhead space for my wheeled luggage before continuing on to my seat with my slightly smaller duffle. I blame the amount of luggage I have on my extended stay, but if I'm telling the truth, I've always been a bit of an overpacker. Turning to slide into the small coach airline seat, I am greeted by a not-so-welcoming but familiar face.

I squeeze my eyes shut, silently willing him to be gone when I open them, knowing almost five hours next to his manspreading legs would only result in a more cramped flight than the already tiny personal space I'd have. When my eyes reopen, he's still sitting there, a smug grin on his face. I watch as he slowly closes his magazine and turns his full attention to me..

"Hello, again, doll. What are the chances," he drawls, running his eyes over me in a way that makes my skin flush, "this should be interesting."

My feet feel stuck to the aisle as I rapidly blink, suddenly aware of just how small the inside of the plane feels with him sharing my personal space. We haven't even left the ground yet, but I wonder if by some strange chance we've already lost cabin pressure with how little air seems to be circulating the cabin. It's not until the woman behind me clears her throat that I finally snap back to the present just as the man stands to allow me a little bit of room to pass to my window seat.

Well, at least he isn't a complete ass that is going to make me *climb* across his lap to get to my seat. Although, he seems like the type that wouldn't altogether mind.

I squeeze just about every muscle in my body tight to make myself smaller and turn so my back is facing his chest as I try to slide past him. I'm momentarily taken aback when our bodies brush against each other, and a sudden zing of energy pulses through every nerve ending of my body. Lowering myself into my seat, I pull my Kindle, headphones, and sketch book from the front pocket of my bag before shoving it under the seat in front of me.

About two hours into the flight, I am finally feeling relaxed enough with the man on my left. He's silently pouring over some documents on his laptop. Thankfully, he hasn't tried to speak with me again, and his legs stay firmly within his own cramped space though our arms occasionally brush against each other in the small space.

Finally settled, I am ready to attempt some much-needed rest. I have never been the type of person to comfortably sleep on a plane; I envy those that can. But today, I am determined to at least get a short nap. I flip the cover over my Kindle and tuck it into the seatback in front of me, open Spotify on my phone while placing my headphones over my ears, and open an acoustic classic rock playlist that I had downloaded before getting on the flight.

Somewhere between the slow sounds of James Taylor and Carole King, I relax further, stretching my legs out in front of me as much as I can while using my duffle bag as a makeshift foot stool. Carole's gentle crooning fills my ears, and that paired with the gyration of the plane easily lull me into an easy sleep.

I have no idea how long I am asleep - my best calculations put it somewhere between two minutes and two hours - before I am shaken. Assuming turbulence, I try to rearrange my body against the window, my eyes remaining closed, and my head on my makeshift pillow. Immediately, I feel the rough movement again, and this time, I realize the sensation isn't turbulence. Instead, a strong hand is on my shoulder, nudging and shaking me to get my attention

Startled when I realize this fact, I sit straight up, removing my feet from my bag and opening my eyes simultaneously. Balking at the man beside me who has the audacity to wake me, I slowly remove my headphones and turn towards him.

"I'm not sure why you felt the need to wake me. Unless there are free drinks or a five course meal being served, please don't do that again."

As I start to place my headphones back on, his hand

comes to my wrist in a gentle movement, freezing me to my spot. My eyes snap back to his, aggravated by his brazen touch that somehow sends electricity coursing through my body. I was right. He *certainly wasn't* used to hearing "no" from females.

"I just thought you would want to know that your bag is making noises," he says, that telltale cat that ate the canary smile spreading back across his face.

My face scrunches in sleep-induced confusion as I try to piece together what he just said. Slowly dropping my headphones back down, my neck cranes towards the duffle bag unceremoniously shoved under the seat like an overfilled sausage in a too small casing.

Listening intently, I know he is right. My bag is making noises. My brain starts doing a quick inventory of everything I had thrown in the duffle bag before I left my Portland apartment this morning. Snacks, a sketch-book, sweatshirt, vibra...FUCK. This wasn't just any noise; it was *vibrating*.

Grumbling, I hoist the bag onto my lap, making quick work of the zipper before diving in with both hands, desperate to quiet the last minute addition to my luggage. I can feel the heat creeping up my cheeks and am confident that I am as pink as my unnatural hair color. It feels like time is standing still, just me, my flustered hands, and the gorgeous yet arrogant stranger curiously darting his eyes between my bag and my face.

A full body pat-down from one of the grumpy TSA agents would have been more pleasant than this. Hell, our plane crashing on a deserted island and having to live out the rest of my days with the cast of Gilligan's Island would be better than this!

"Fuck!"

Through pursed lips, the word comes out louder than I had intended, causing my seat to be kicked by the woman with a small child in the row behind me. Jerking back into my seat from the impact, my hands unintentionally slip out of the bag with the noisy culprit literally in hand.

Two

Nico

IF MY EYES are the size of saucers, hers are the size of old-fashioned carnival Ferris wheels. Her eyes are darting back and forth between my eyes and the sparkly, purple vibrator in her hand. I watch as her skin pales before morphing into a shade of pink usually reserved for cotton candy..

I originally noticed her when she sauntered through the terminal, dropping into the chair across from me. Immediately, it was as if I was drawn to her by something unnatural. I couldn't stop staring as she scrolled through her phone, busying her lip between her teeth, and suddenly squeaking as she did an adorable little chair dance. I won't lie; she instantly made me hard. When she stepped next to me on the plane several minutes later and stared at me with stunned, cat-like green eyes, I realized she was serendipitously going to be seated next to me for several hours.

She fiddles with a button on the side of the device, first turning it to warp speed before finally silencing the toy. I'm not sure which is more hysterical; her sitting with the now quiet toy in her hand or the look on her face as she stares straight ahead at the seatback in front of her.

I can't help it. I try, but a thunderous laugh tears out of my chest making my entire body shake. I continue to laugh as she hastily throws the vibrator back into her bag like it is too hot to hold in her hand a second longer. I have never been one to laugh until I cry, but as I continue laughing, a few honest to goodness tears leak from my eyes.

She turns towards me, her dark irises dilating in swirls of yellows and greens. Her mouth parts as if she is going to speak before quickly closing once again as she jerks her body back, now parallel to the seat in front of her again.

Still in the throes of what can only be described as a very unmanly fit of giggles, I turn to her, trying to profusely apologize while being shushed by the passengers around us.

"Stop," she says, almost pleading.

I offer another apology, my hands coming up in front of my chest as a show of goodwill before silence settles between us again. No more than thirty seconds pass before I find myself laughing again. When her head snaps back to me, fire in those gorgeous eyes, I stop, feeling my pants tighten around my crotch again. I mumble, "there is nothing to be ashamed of. It's good to have a healthy appetite for pleasure."

Her face flushes again, her head falling into her hands.

"I am..." she stumbles on her words, "I am *beyond* mortified."

I could tell from the moment I saw her at the airport and from the way she spoke to me when I first tried to tell her what was happening in her luggage that she was feisty. I know I am pushing the limits, but trying to lessen her embarrassment, I lean in as close as I can with the armrest between us and speak in a low voice, ensuring no one else could hear.

"You showed me yours. Would it make it better if I showed you mine now?"

She guffaws, earning us another shush from the other passengers who were certainly having a less entertaining flight than I was. She finally appears to be slowly relaxing as I hold out my hand towards her.

"Nico," I say.

Reluctantly, she slides her hand into mine, her long slim fingers sending vibrations through my body. "Mina," she tentatively supplies.

Was she feeling this electricity, too? She had to be.

As we slowly separate hands, the flight attendant appears, pushing a drink cart down the aisle. "Let me buy you a drink to make up for laughing." She tries to shake her head, but I gently touch her wrist which had fallen to the armrest between us. An earnest yet shy smile laces her lips.

"No buying a drink required," she says to me before looking towards the flight attendant, "but, I would *love* a cup of coffee. Black, two sugars."

I pass her the coffee she orders with the two individual sugar packets before taking the Bloody Mary I requested from the attendant. Hell, if it was only past nine A.M. when we left Portland a few hours ago, it had to be close to noon by now with the way time changed as we crossed the country.

Testing the waters to see if her walls remained down, I looked over at her. "You sure are a cheap date."

She laughs, almost spitting her coffee out.

Surprising me, she holds her styrofoam cup of coffee up to my can of beer. "To cheap dates and entertainingly embarrassing flights."

I repeat her words and ceremoniously tap her airline

branded Styrofoam cup with mine before we each take long drinks from our respective beverages.

Normally, I tend to keep to myself. But with her- with Mina- I feel this ridiculous urge to keep talking, to keep *her* talking. I wanted, no...I *needed* to know more about her.

"So, Portland. Home or vacation?"

She lets out a long sigh, and I'm secretly hoping she says vacation and that just maybe, our end destination is the same.

"Home," she says as I slowly feel myself deflating. "At least, it was."

I feel my curiosity returning as she continues.

"I'm honestly not sure anymore. It's been home for the last few years, but some family issues are bringing me back to the east coast. I'm not sure what the end game is yet. How about you?"

Finishing my drink, I continue our conversation. "Portland? Just visiting my sister who is in college there. Don't get me wrong; it's a gorgeous place, but the whole 'Keep Portland Weird' thing is just a little...well...weird to me."

She laughs. "That's kinda the point, and you're right; it *is* beautiful. So much beautiful nature, gorgeous hiking, an arts community like no other, recreational use is legal..." She trails off at that last point, tilting her head back and forth. Her passion is evident when she speaks. Fuck, it makes her even sexier.

Mina beams when she talks about Portland, almost like a proud mother talking about their toddler taking their first steps. She pulls out her phone, swiping across a few photos and showing me some of her favorite places to hike. As she continues swiping across pictures, several shots of tattoos flood by, each in various states of completion.

"Sorry about that," she shies away, pulling her phone back to her chest.

But she had nothing to be shy about. Over her long sleeves and pants, I couldn't tell if she had any ink of her own, but it wouldn't surprise me if she did. From what I can tell, there is nothing traditional about Mina. Her nose, slightly upturned, was adorned with the tiniest stud in her right nostril. Her hair, almost down to the middle of her back, fell in loose waves of bright pink

Inquiring, I ask if they were hers.

"Yes and no." She shrugs. "I mean, they're not *on* me, but they are mine. It's kinda what I do for a living."

My God. She was gorgeous, liked the outdoors, was family-oriented, and made a living as a tattoo artist. And from the pictures I was only afforded a glance of, she was good. Really good.

I can't help myself, and once again, being in this

woman's presence makes my mouth and brain operate separate from one another.

"What's the catch?"

She stares at me quizzically.

"I'm sorry if I'm being forward. I just...what's the catch? You're fucking gorgeous, clearly talented as hell, and it sounds like you care a great deal for your family. Are you married? Celibate? A lesbian?"

She laughs, her cheeks flushing to that near perfect pink I remembered from earlier, and I suddenly wonder if her nipples match the flush of her cheeks when she is embarrassed.

"Not married. Not interested in women except for a few instances in college. Not celibate. Well, at least, not by choice. But don't you worry about that, Nico," she says as she lightly pats my arm with her hand. "Clearly, you've already learned that isn't anything I can't handle on my own."

I laugh, and a small grin breaks out across her face as the pilot comes over the loudspeaker announcing our descent into the Charlotte airport.

She continues, "Enough of that, though. You said you were visiting Portland. Where are you headed home to?"

I tell her that Charlotte is home, and something in her eyes sparkles. She tells me she will only be about a half hour away. I know that I already have to see her again and we aren't even off the fucking plane.

We taxi the runway, and I reach for the sketchbook she had placed in the seatback pocket earlier. Taking a pen from my own bag, I flip the cover, find a blank page, and scrawl my number down before handing it back to her.

"I know you're a cheap date, but regardless, since I know you'll be staying so close, I'd love to take you out for a real date."

She captures that bottom lip of hers between her teeth and gives me a slow nod. "I think I'd like that."

I tell her she knows how to get in touch with me while handing her the sketchpad. Then, I help her with her overhead luggage and walk side by side through the terminal with her towards baggage claim. It strangely feels natural and I have the urge to grasp her hand but don't. How have I known this woman for only a few hours, and I already don't want to let her go? Actually, I'd like to do the very opposite - maybe tie her to my bed and explore every inch of her body with my tongue.

I slightly shake my head to clear those thoughts as I sadly lead her out to her Uber. We shake hands before we part, though I wanted to do so much more. After her Uber drives off, I walk towards the long-term parking garage, the slight scent of sandalwood infiltrates my nostrils, wafting in the air around me.

I never thought to ask her for her number, somehow convinced she felt our connection, too, and would choose to call me. But now that she isn't in front of me, I am starting to doubt our chemistry.

Damnit, she better call.

Three

MINA

I am barely out of my Uber when two girls and a small ball of fluff come careening down the stairs of the house they share with their father and grandmother, almost throwing themselves into my arms. Now fifteen and twelve, it had been several years since I last saw my nieces, and they are every bit the teenagers I expected to see in front of me. Helping with my overweight luggage, they walk me towards the front door and into the large foyer of the Victorian house which had been almost completely remodeled since my last visit.

Gorgeous, original hardwood floors played center-piece to neutral walls. A staircase to the right leads to an open loft on the second floor which is flanked with bedrooms. Family pictures dote the walls along the staircase. The girls, dropping my luggage at the base of the staircase, run through the hallway, loudly announcing my arrival to not only our house, but probably also to everyone else in Johnson Creek. Hanging up the light sweater I had traveled with and used as a makeshift pillow on the plane, I follow the sounds into the kitchen, only then also becoming aware of the delicious aroma of a traditional, home-cooked Greek dinner.

My mother, fondly referred to as Pauli by her friends, gestures for her younger granddaughter to take over stirring a large pot on the stove before coming over to me and lovingly patting my cheek.

"It's been too long since you've been home, Philly."

I grimace at the nickname, a shortening of my full name, Philomena, before wrapping my mother in a long hug. "I know, but I'm here now and here for as long as you, Colin, and the girls need me, Mom."

My mom is a short lady, fitting snugly under the arms of my own 5' 7" frame. Her neatly coiffed gray hair tickles my chin as I hold her in my arms, inhaling her familiar scent of vanilla and coconut. She has used the same perfume since I was a child, some knock-off name-brand bottle my father picked up for her late one Christmas on his way home from work. It was a last minute purchase but had been a staple of her daily life ever since.

As we end our embrace, a door off the kitchen opens, and my brother enters the room. "Hey, Philly! I don't remember the last time I was so happy to see you."

I smile as he pulls me into another familiar hug, dropping his hands to my shoulders as he looks into my eyes. I can see the pain in his eyes along with his silent gratitude.

After dinner, the girls sit around the table working on school projects with my mom while Colin and I sit on the massive, wooden deck off the family room. Their dog, Stella, sniffs around the fenced-in backyard. After sitting in silence for several minutes, he sighs. "I know I haven't said it since you've gotten here, but thank you, Philly; I mean it. Between the girls, Mom, and work, I feel like I haven't had a second to myself in the last three months."

I pat his hand with mine while giving him a small nod. "I'm here now, Colin. I'm so sorry it couldn't be sooner."

I wanted to be there when my mom called and told me about Tabitha's diagnosis and again at her subsequent death. I wanted to be there for the funeral and wanted to be there in the days immediately following, but an overly controlling boyfriend hell bent on ruining my life kept me away. My family knew how Matt had treated me, though not to the full extent. That was something I wanted to keep from them.

My whirlwind relationship with Matt had started almost a year prior after we were introduced by a mutual friend. He was sweet, loving, and beyond caring. But he was also mean, threatening, and sometimes downright scary. Hateful words were often thrown at me, but the night those words turned into a shove and resulted in a black eye, I knew it was time to walk away from him before he had the chance to do something worse. The very next day, Colin had texted asking for help. So, I booked my plane ticket back to Johnson Creek with the help of Daphne, making my quick escape. I was just thankful that the ugly yellow bruise had healed enough to easily be concealed with foundation, saving me from having to tell my family the entire story.

Now sitting here with my brother, listening to the sounds of the kids inside with my mom through the screen door, I couldn't help but know that I had made the right choice.

"I'm serious. I'm here to do whatever you need." Giving my brother a playful push, I continued, "Remember when we were kids and you always made me pretend to be the maid for you and Timothy O'Neil while you played video games?"

He chuckles a little at the memory. "Yeah, because all sixteen-year-olds needed a maid to bring them Mountain Dew and Cheetos when they were playing video games all day. You always wanted to be where I was, and I felt bad pushing you away. At least this way, I was able to include you, too."

I smile at his admission.

"Well, consider this your chance to use my services however you need, good sir." I say with a horrible British accent. "Grocery shopping, getting the girls ready for school, getting Mom out of the house for a few hours..."

Colin laughs again. As wonderfully supportive as our mother can be, she can be equally as overbearing. I took the brunt of it growing up with my multicolored hair, love of tattoos, and equal love of the wrong boys. Colin, on the other hand, had a well-respected job, the girls, and until recently, a wife my mother loved as her own daughter.

As if on cue, he reaches for the drink he had sitting on the small table between our chairs and takes a long gulp from it before setting it back down among the condensation.

"She tried to set me up on a date last week."

Rarely at a loss for words, I stumble over what to say, my eyes growing wider as I try to comprehend what my brother just told me. "Oh, Colin, she didn't?!"

His shoulders start to shake, not from tears but from laughter. His eyes - the same shade as mine - crinkle and for the first time since I arrived home, I can see how the years have caught up with him. The lines around his eyes are just a little deeper and more pronounced than the last time I was home. His hair, previously thick and raven black, is now flecked with gray.

We sit there for several more minutes, randomly breaking out into fits of giggles before I notice the amused glint in his eyes has suddenly departed and sadness has taken up the vacancy.

"I just miss her so fucking much."

Standing up, I begrudgingly pull him to his feet, wrapping my arms around him. "I know you do. And seriously, next time tell Mom to fuck off. You're on your own timetable, not hers."

He squeezes back once more before picking up his drink, walking towards the door with Stella prancing behind him. "See ya tomorrow, sis. Thanks for being here."

I follow my brother into the house a few minutes later, depositing my empty glass into the dishwasher, and find my way upstairs to the guest bedroom which would become mine for the foreseeable future. Flopping onto the double bed, I pull my phone from my pocket to find a text from my best friend, now on the opposite side of the country instead of a few blocks away. It makes my heart pang with sadness.

Daphne: *I miss you already*

Fingers flying over the phone's keyboard, I fire off a return text, thrilled to see three dots dancing on the bottom of the screen almost immediately.

Me: *I miss you more! You will not believe what happened on my flight.*

Daphne: *Tell. Me. Everything!*

Me: *Well, should I start with the absolute yummy looking asshole who turned out to be super sweet as well as my seatmate or would you prefer I start with the part where I accidentally turned on my vibrator that was in my bag with my feet while I napped and then PULLED IT OUT OF MY BAG IN FRONT OF HIM.*

Three dots dance on the bottom of the screen and then disappear several times before my phone rings, startling me. I answer the incoming FaceTime call from Daphne and find her on the other end all but rocking with laughter.

"A *vibrator!*" she howls with laughter.

I shush her before I prop my phone up against a pillow. After making sure we can see each other, I drop my head into my hands, laughing right alongside Daphne.

"It was *mortifying,* Daph! You have *no* idea!"

"How is it that things like this always seem to happen to you? Remember the time you fell off the bar doing karaoke after the shop's Christmas party? Or the time you spent almost an entire first date walking around Downtown Portland with a strand of toilet paper trailing behind you from your shoe?"

Oh, how could I forget? Daphne wasn't lying. Embarrassing moments were always lurking around the corner, waiting for the perfect opportunity to sneak into my life. I cringe, and as she sees my face, she quickly changes the subject from the vibrator fiasco to Nico, my seatmate and man who had the pleasure of being present for the aforementioned fiasco.

I tell her about my first impression of Nico, sitting across from me in the airport, how he both pissed me off and made me want to run my hands over his broad chest at the same time. I told her about his sexy eyes, peeks of ink that swirled from around his neckline and up his neck, and smattering of gray hair around his closely cut temples. We talk about my utter shock when I realized we would be sitting next to each other for hours, and about how we were continually shushed by other passengers around us when we couldn't stop laughing, about how he offered to buy me an overpriced plane drink, and how he lived just a short drive away in Charlotte.

"Please tell me you're going to see him again," she almost pleads with me.

I sigh. "I'm not sure, Daph. He did give me his number and asked if he could take me out for a proper drink, butI'm just not sure. I'm here because Colin needs me, not to have a fling with some guy I barely know. Especially after Matt. I don't even know this man."

I pull out my sketchbook from the duffle bag I had haphazardly tossed on the bed earlier, flipping to the page where Nico wrote his number. Instinctively, my fingers trace the letters of his name and the numbers on the page. Normally, I would be horrified if anyone so carelessly picked up my sketchbook and scrawled a phone number in it, but for some strange reason, I'm not bothered by Nico doing exactly that. I can feel the indentation of each character on the page, ironically feeling like he had already made an impression on me, just as he did on the page.

I could see Daphne rolling her eyes at me across the phone screen. "Mina, listen to me. Sure, you're there for your brother, but you also packed up your life and flew across the country for him with no time constraint. And Matt - don't even get me started on that complete asshat. Not all men are like him, Mina. Just because you're there for Colin doesn't mean you can't be there for you, too."

I tell her I would consider it to appease her, and we chat for a few more minutes before promising to catch up again soon. Hanging up, I stand from the bed, suddenly aware of how exhausted I am. I unzip my luggage, desperate to get into some comfortable pajamas. Catching a glance of myself in the mirror, I can't help but see just how tired I look. My hair was beginning to fade, I had circles under my eyes from hours of travel, and my skin looked dull. How long had I looked like this? It looked like I had aged ten years in ten hours.

———

I WAKE THE FOLLOWING MORNING, AND FOR A FEW seconds, I am startled when my sleep-filled eyes take in the room around me. Slowly regaining my bearings, I stretch out in the to- small-for me bed, limbs all but spilling off the sides. Reaching for my phone, I'm surprised to find it was already after ten in the morning, and aside from the small sounds coming from Stella, the house was quiet.

Padding down the stairs in search of coffee, I remember that my mom had left for a day trip with a local women's club she had joined after my father died.

The ladies of Johnson Creek take their socializing seriously, and along with weekly lunches, they often travel to neighboring cities to visit museums or see shows that were on national tours. She had drastically cut down her trips since Tabitha died and she moved in with Colin, but with me being back for less than 24 hours, she must have felt like she could finally regain her status of top Johnson Creek socialite. I had promised Colin I'd be home when the girls arrived back from school, and hearing so, my mom had jumped at the chance to sneak off to whatever adventure awaited her and her friends.

Pouring a mug of coffee from a freshly brewed pot, I take myself back upstairs to the bathroom I was now sharing with two adolescent girls. Hair care products and accessories cover the counter. A flat iron is still plugged in and turned on. Cracked makeup palettes are strewn about as if in the middle of a war zone. A faded Minnie Mouse shower curtain hangs from the tub, sending a silent reminder through my body of just how much time I had missed out on with these girls.

Fingering the items on the counter, I come across an avocado face mask and immediately decide that since I have the house to myself, I would start with a little bit of self-care. Then, I decide that when Colin comes home from work, I am going to ask him if I can enlist the girls to help redecorate their bathroom into something more befitting for their age. It wasn't much, but it was a start on rebuilding a relationship with both girls, and honestly, I just didn't know how long I could tolerate the watchful eye of Minnie Mouse judging me.

I slather the thick, green sludge of the mask onto my face before grabbing a bottle of hair color out of my luggage and walking it back into the bathroom. Next to Daphne, the person I would miss most in Portland was my hair stylist. She had my signature bright pink color down to a science, and before leaving, had premixed a bottle for me as a going away present.

Standing in the bathroom in a tiny pair of shorts and a too small camisole that I don't mind getting hair color on, I plunge the bottle into my hair, being extra cautious around my forehead and ears. Hearing my phone ping from the next room, I look down to find that my hands are now completely covered in pink. Lord help me if this stains the tub as bad as it has my hands. Now I know why Sylvia, my stylist, always swore on wearing two pairs of gloves.

I continue the best I can, squirting globs of color into my hair and pulling it down through my long strands. I finish, plopping the now color soaked hair in a large pile on the top of my head. I wash my hands, looking down to see they still have a pink tinge to them. Splotches of pink dot my camisole.

Trying to contain as much of what could only be described as the aftermath of a *My Little Pony* explosion, I startle when the doorbell rings from downstairs.

"Just a minute," I yell as I throw the color bottle into the trash.

The doorbell rings again.

Growing as impatient as the person on the other side of the door, I plod down the stairs in all my masked and hair colored glory. "On my way!"

Flinging the door open, I stare back in horror as my eyes move from the ground, up past muscular, denim-clad legs and a broad chest, and straight into the eyes of the man who I had horrified myself in front of less than a full day prior.

My voice comes out as nothing more than a raspy gasp as I try to hide behind the front door while Stella betrays me and runs towards him before circling his feet.

"Nico?"

Four

Nico

THE TINY DOG runs in figure eights around my feet, but instead of bending to pacify it, I stare straight ahead into the eyes of the woman I left behind at the airport parking garage.

She has green goop on her face that is starting to dry and crack, and she is covered from the tips of her ears to the top of her head in some pink substance I can only assume is hair color. If it wasn't for those huge, yellow-green eyes staring at me, the same wide eyed look as when she pulled a vibrator from her bag on a packed flight, I would second guess that it is actually Mina.

My eyes wander the length of her body. She is now wearing much less than she was on the plane. God, she is perfect. Even covered in all that shit. Long legs lead to gorgeous, thick thighs that are barely covered by small, black cotton shorts. A thin strip of her stomach is show-ing, and a scarcely there white tank leaves little to the imagination. Her breasts strain against the material, and without a bra between the shirt and her skin, I can make out the outline of her nipples as they pebble against the shirt. My assumption about her having tattoos had been correct. I can now see beautiful swirls of colorful ink running the length of both arms. A full-sleeve of beau-tiful florals and small, woodland creatures envelopes her left arm. An almost abstract design stretches from her wrist to her shoulder on her right arm. Immediately, my dick twitches in my pants making my jeans tighter while I imagine tracing each design with my tongue. I wonder where else she is hiding artwork on her body, and even with all the shit on her head and face, I want to throw her against the nearest wall and strip her bare to find out.

I only come back to earth when she speaks.

"Nico? What...what are you doing at my brother's house?"

As she speaks, I can hear the sound of a door opening in the rear of the house and footprints follow, coming closer to us.

Colin comes into view before busting out with loud laughter. "Hell, sis, you look like one of the girl's science fair projects gone bad. Thanks for grabbing the door. Hey, Nicolas! Come on in, man!"

Mina looks between me and her brother several times before turning, quickly retreating up the stairs.

"Mina!" I can't help myself. Her name crosses my lips before my brain has the chance to catch up.She completely ignores me.

Colin looks at me quizzically before tentatively speaking as he moves for me to make my way into his home.

"You know my sister?"

Fuck, my mind spins. Mina is Colin's sister.

We make our way into the kitchen, and I take a seat at the large island surrounded on one side by tall kitchen stools. Grabbing two beers from the refrigerator, Colin passes one to me across the island then continues to stare, waiting for an answer.

"No. Well, I mean...yes?"

Skeptically laughing, he asks which it was.

I tell Colin how I had met her the day before, leaving out the details of how she immediately made me hard and the part about her battery-operated toy. I tell him how I first saw her in the airport terminal and was then surprised to be seated next to her on the flight.

"I knew you had a sister, but I never thought she

would look like *that*, man." Colin glares before I quickly add, "You know, the complete opposite of you."

If Mina was wild and free, her brother was put together and reserved. The man had his initials embroidered on the sleeves of his dress shirts, and I was fairly confident that he owned at least one sweater vest. We had met several years earlier when he and his wife were touring homes to buy and despite our drastically different appearances, we had hit it off. We had grown close since then, with his girls even calling me Uncle Nico.

"I always thought you would get along well with her," he says nonchalantly.

I laugh and ask why he never introduced us before. He responds by telling me he rarely sees her, only speaking to her a few times each week until she agreed to come back home last week. It feels weird, almost like he is giving me his blessing to do all the naughty things I've been thinking about over the last day.

We chat about the possibility of hosting an event to honor Tabitha and about the house I had purchased a few months prior with hopes of flipping. We speak about the girls and how they are coping with the loss of their mother. I had lost my parents when I was young, so to some extent, I can understand the ups and downs they were both experiencing.

While trying to focus on our conversation, my mind still continues to stray to the beautiful enigma of the woman upstairs. It had only been one day, but I had expected her to text me immediately and was bummed when she hadn't. I didn't have trouble when it came to women and had my fair share of one night stands to warm my bed at night after a failed marriage when I was younger. I never wanted for a woman, and they called when I gave them my number. They always called. So, when she didn't immediately do so, I had all but given up hope of seeing her again. Seeing her open that door today had felt serendipitous. That is, until the realization set in that she was also my best friend's sister.

As if I had willed her to appear, I hear her come down the stairs. Tentatively, she walks into the kitchen, glancing between me and her brother. She is now dressed in slim jeans that hug her luscious thighs and a deep-purple tee that make her eyes even more vibrant. Her hair is in loose, damp waves around her shoulders, and she has a light coating of pink gloss on her lips.

Colin breaks the silence first. "So, I see you've already met the illustrious Nicolas, my best friend."

Her eyes widen before she slowly nods. Moving to the counter behind the island, she reaches for a travel mug before filling it to the top with coffee and sugar.

Colin's phone rings and he excuses himself to speak with a client. All the while, her back remains to me.

"Mina."

She slowly turns to look at me, cheeks rosy with embarrassment. A long sigh escapes her lips. "I honestly didn't expect to ever see you again."

That kind of stings.

"I was hoping you would call."

An unsettled smile pulls at the corner of her lips, making her mouth quirk into an adorable half-smile while sadness flashes in her eyes. As if waiting for its cue, my dick jumps in my jeans again.

She lifts her mug to her pouty lips and takes a long drink from the cup before coughing and pouring the rest down the drain. "Ugh, it's cold and tastes old."

Colin walks back in then, looking flustered and apologizes while picking up his briefcase to tackle an emergency meeting at his office. "Feel free to stick around and finish your drink, Nicolas, but I've gotta run and take care of this. Philly, you good?"

She simply nods in response as her brother walks out the back door.

Before my mind can catch up to my legs, I stand and walk to Mina. She appears reluctant at first, stepping back until she is flush with the kitchen counter. While I want to immediately lift her onto the countertop and devour her, I don't want to scare her away. Instead, I instinctively take her hand in mine. Energy courses through my body. Fuck, what was this woman doing to me?

"Have coffee with me?"

She takes her hand from mine, and I feel empty. "I shouldn't. I mean, I can't."

Our eyes meet, and I know mine are silently pleading with hers. "You can't, or you won't?"

"Nico," my name on her lips is intoxicating, "I'm sure you're a fantastic guy. But things are difficult for me, and I mean," she stutters before continuing, "you're friends with my *brother*."

I reach my hand back out to her, and I can hear the desperation in my voice when I speak. "Just one cup- my treat. Besides, yours is all down the drain."

She sighs long and hard before letting out a small laugh and shrugs. Painfully slow, she steps towards me and slides her hand into mine, her slim fingers curling around my own digits.

"Just one cup?"

I nod.

We settle on Dina's Diner a few blocks from Colin's house, and in lieu of driving my truck, decide to walk in the warm, late-spring air. While we walk, her hand surprisingly still in mine, I reveal how Colin and I had met and grown close. I talk with her about her nieces, Emily and Laurel, and tell her how they rave about her.

She giggles. "They just like me because I'm not their father. I swear, my brother has no idea how to have fun."

I laugh. I had heard Colin talk about Mina over the few years I had known him, but he only ever called her Philly. I hadn't ever noticed pictures of her in his home, and honestly, I never expected her to be as dynamic as she was. With Colin as a brother, I all but expected a straight-laced, beige-cardigan-wearing librarian type, the very antithesis of Mina

I only release her hand to open the door for her when we make it to the restaurant. Thanks to it being a Wednesday afternoon, the diner is only sparsely filled, and we easily grab a booth near the back. Our server comes over and shrieks when she looks at Mina, drawing the attention of the few other restaurant patrons.

"Oh. My. God," the woman punctuates each word. "When did you get back into town?"

Mina laughs, a full on belly laugh that I didn't expect to come from her slim yet curvy body. Standing, she warmly hugs the woman, telling her she returned to Johnson Creek yesterday.

She introduces me to the woman and I learn that her name is Steph and that the two women were friends throughout their adolescent years. She takes our drink orders and hurries away, bringing back two cups of coffee just a short time after. Declining food, I watch as Mina rips open sugar packets before ceremoniously dumping them into her cup and slowly stirring.

We are talking for a few minutes when Steph comes back and places two slices of peanut butter pie on our table. "On the house," she says while giving Mina a wink.

Mina takes a bite of the pie and groans almost sexually while she slowly pulls the fork from her lips. Still holding my fork in my hand, my eyes are transfixed on her lips as I feel the familiar tightening of my cock against my jeans.

She breaks the silence while pointing to my plate. "You better eat yours before I get my hands on your slice, too."

I quickly snap my eyes back to hers as laughter overtakes her. "Guess you're pretty serious about your pie, eh?"

"Best pie on the east coast," she responds.

We continue to eat while getting to know each other. I learn that she would be picking up a guest artist residency at a local tattoo shop, that she co-owns her own shop in Portland, and that she didn't have any definite timetable on returning to Portland. That last bit of information makes me hopeful.

Glancing at the time, Mina notices it is almost time for the girls to return from school. She decides that we should get back to the house, unaware if Colin would be back from his emergency meeting before they arrive home. I pay for our drinks and leave a generous tip while Mina swaps numbers with Steph and says her goodbyes.

When we arrive back at the house, we stand on the front porch, and I once again take her hands in mine.

"I know I said one cup, but if you ever decide that one cup wasn't enough, you still have my number."

She smiles, a sigh coming from her lips. "You're my brother's best friend, Nico. You seem wonderful; you really do. I just..." she trails off. "I just don't want to come between the two of you, especially now when he needs our support more than ever."

I release her hands and slowly brush her hair behind her ear, laughing when I notice that the tip of her ear is still stained pink from her hair color. She quickly tries to cover her ear with her hair to hide the stain.

I want to kiss her. God, how I want to grab her by the waist and pull her into me, to run my hands through her hair. Slowly, I move towards her, ready to make my move despite her protest. Hell, if it did bother Colin, he would get over it.

Her pupils dilate, and her lips slowly part. She

could say it was because of her brother all she wanted, but I knew girls like Mina before - strong and capable women who always choose the wrong men. And I knew she had been through hell with those other disgusting members of the male species just like the women I had known in my past. I knew she wanted me as much as I wanted her. As much as she made excuses, her body defied her words, leading me to believe she wouldn't resist.

Just before my hands can reach her waist, before our lips can crash together, a yellow school bus pulls up in front of the house, making Mina jump back.

Frustrated, I grit out, "cockblocked by two kids. Damn."

Mina laughs at me as the girls run up to the door. They take turns giving me hugs before moving to hug their aunt. She unlocks the door before ushering the girls into the house, leaving us alone again.

We stare at each other for a long while before she breaks the silence first. "Thanks for the coffee, Nico." Although tall herself, she pushes herself up to her tiptoes before gently placing her lips against my cheek.

Turning around, she walks into the house, the door closing behind her.

Five

MINA

I wake Thursday morning with a smile on my face. Last night, I spoke at length with Daphne and decided that although everything logical in my brain said to leave Nico alone, that maybe she was right. Maybe it was okay to pursue something casual with him. Despite my unknown future in Johnson Creek and the even more absurd fact that he was my brother's best friend, just *maybe* it would be okay if we spent some time together. It could be fun. And Lord knew I needed some fun in my life after Matt.

Even though I had known Nico for less than 48 hours, when I was with him, he made me feel beautiful, protected, and desired - a far cry from the men in my past.

I hear the doorbell ring downstairs, and a few moments later, my mom calls to me from the bottom of the steps.

"Philly, my girl, there is a delivery here for you!"

I'm not expecting something, but knowing Daphne, who was always up to something crazy, I fully expect whatever has arrived would be both from her and totally embarrassing. I mean, the girl once had a bag of dicks delivered to me on my birthday. Not actual dicks, of course, but a giant bag of gummy penises attached to balloons of an equally phallic nature. We snacked on different colors and flavors of gummy dicks for weeks at the shop.

Pulling on a ratty old robe, I descend the stairs to find my mom holding the largest flower display that I have ever seen. My mom is dwarfed behind the vase of tulips, gerbera daisies, and yellow roses. Greenery cascades down the sides of the vase, and baby's breath is tucked between the blooms.

Taking the arrangement from my mother, I carry it into the kitchen, setting it on the island before taking the small card from within the bunch. Opening it, I notice my fingers are slightly trembling. A simple request was scrawled across the card.

Just one more cup?

-N

My mom eyes me suspiciously, and I can't help but giggle while I try to stifle it by biting my lip. While she didn't see us together yesterday, the girls were more than happy to tell her about coming home to school to find, in their words, 'Aunt Mina and Uncle Nico together on the front porch looking like they were in love.'

"My girl, just be careful with that one."

Halfheartedly heeding her warning, I give her a wary smile before snapping a picture of the beautiful bouquet and returning upstairs to my bedroom while she takes the flowers to the kitchen table. Phone still in hand, I debate texting Daphne but decide against it because of the time difference. I love my best friend, but to say she is not a morning person is putting it lightly. Instead, I find myself looking at Nico's number in my sketchbook. Before I can talk myself out of it, I attach the picture of the flowers to a new message and hit send along with one word.

Me: *Okay.*

I STAND IN FRONT OF THE ENTRANCE TO BROKEN Sparrow, taking in a deep breath before pulling it open. My eyes wander over the gorgeous pictures on the wall of artwork that has been created in this shop over the years, and for one moment, I feel out of my league. Some of the biggest names in my industry have held resident and guest spots in this very building, and knowing I'm about to start mine leaves me feeling humbled.

Continuing to walk through the shop, I make my way to the desk where I am greeted by a young girl, probably in her early 20's, who introduces herself to me as Raven. Her hair is various shades of purples and blues, pulled into a bun on top of her head with the sides closely trimmed and an intricate design shaved into the short hair. Her nose has a stud on each side, her lip is pierced, and when she speaks, I note that she also has her tongue pierced. Bright colors swirl on her eyelids, and meticulously drawn eyeliner rims her ocean-blue eyes. Immediately, I know I am going to like her.

She calls out to Thom, and he rolls himself out of an office before waving me back. He pages through my portfolio while we chat about everything from my background to artists we admired and shop policies. We decide it is best for me to start small by opening up appointments at the shop for two days each week

I had grown a large social media following over the years, mostly due to my artwork with the occasional selfie thrown in for good measure. With my followers spanning the globe, we both expect I will quickly be able to fill my books and expand to more days as needed.

Through our discussion, I learn that Thom is in his mid-fifties, though he looks younger, and that he had taken over Broken Sparrow three years earlier from his dad, who had taken it over from his dad before that. He has a son that goes to the same school as Colin's girls and is around their age, and he and his wife had married right out of high school. He insists he isn't an artist himself and is only there for the business side of Broken Sparrow. It was his goal to retire before he was too old to enjoy life with his son and wife, and I admired a man who could admit that.

Before leaving the shop, I speak more with Raven, giving her my number in case she needed to reach out to me for any appointments or had any questions. She gives me a big, toothy grin as she texts me so I could save her number in my phone as well. I retrace my steps to the front of the shop, and once outside, I snap a selfie in front of the door that is decorated with the Broken Sparrow logo.

Climbing into my mom's car which she had graciously offered to lend me today, I pull up my Instagram and post the photo.

My new home away from home @BrokenSparrow-Tattoo! Can't wait to see you there!

Feeling positively giddy, I arrive home in time to help my mom cook dinner. Mostly, she orders me around while she takes control of the operation and delegates simple tasks to me, like chopping vegetables for a salad.

As we sit around the table after dinner - me, Mom, Colin, and the girls - I tell them about my day at Broken Sparrow. The girls instantly think it is the coolest thing ever and beg to come see me at the shop. Colin reluctantly gives in only after I lovingly convince him that the girls would come home without any body modifications. I may be his little sister, but I'm not enough of a brat to put ink on the skin of his underage daughters, and he knows it.

The girls clear the table, and Mom heads into the kitchen to store the leftovers, leaving Colin and I alone. Absentmindedly, he pulls the card from the flowers. He reads it before tossing it on the table next to my bouquet. I feel a pang of protectiveness over the simple paper card and right it back between the beautiful blossoms.

"You and Nicolas, eh?"

I groan. "It was just coffee."

He rolls his eyes and they shift back to the flowers before falling back to mine.

I want to ask him what my mother meant earlier when she told me to be careful with him. I want to ask him why it matters to him that Nico had sent me flowers, but part of me already knows it was because he was protecting his little sister while also mourning his own relationship. If I was going to pursue something with Nico, I realize I would have to tread carefully around my brother.

Standing to walk past him, I pat him on the shoulder, and he places one hand over mine.

"He's a good guy"

I'm confused by my brother and think about what he just said as I walk into the living room, settling into an oversized chair with my sketchbook in hand and headphones over my ears. The Lumineers sing while my pencil works over the paper quickly, my hand seeming to move separately from my brain. Even with the girls eventually joining me in the room, I zone out and work, my mind continually veering back to Nico - how his hand felt in mine, how easy it was to laugh around him, the mischievous way he looked at me while I held my fork in my mouth.

My phone lights up on the small side table. Unlocking the screen, I eagerly open my messages to find one word staring back at me on the screen.

Nico: *When?*

His eagerness to see me makes me smile. Matt only ever wanted me when it was convenient for him. With

Nico, I feel like a priority, and we barely know each other. It is...refreshing.

Me: *I'm watching the girls tomorrow night, but am free on Saturday?*

Nico: *I'll pick you up at 10. Dress comfortably. Wear sneakers.*

Me: *Ten at night?! That's like, way past my bedtime!*

Nico: *No, ten in the morning. You'll like it. Trust me.*

A date with Nico- at ten in the morning. Suddenly, I feel like I made the wrong decision putting my faith into whatever this thing was that was growing between us. I place my phone back on the side table, again picking up my pencil in its place. Only then do I look down at what my hands were drawing.

Staring back at me is a portrait of a man with dark swirling eyes, beautiful full lips, and just the hint of a tattoo crawling up the side of his neck.

I had drawn Nico.

Six

NICO

I ARRIVE at Colin's house a few minutes before ten on Saturday morning and am pleased to find Mina already on the front porch. As she scampers down the walkway towards my truck, I quickly exit and walk around to the passenger side of the vehicle to open the door for her. Surprisingly, before grabbing the handle inside the truck and hoisting herself to the seat, she gently reaches around my neck and gives me a hug, pressing herself against my chest. This woman is made to be held against my body. Every curve of hers fitting perfectly with mine. I bite back a groan and she lowers herself against my body.

Reclaiming my position in the driver's seat, I turn to look at her, my heart nearly bursting in my chest as a huge smile crosses her lips. She wears tight yoga pants that cling to the curves of her lower half and an equally curve hugging tank that pushes her breasts together, highlighting her ample cleavage. She's fucking gorgeous and I have the sudden urge to stay parked right here and stare at her all damn day. Her hair is piled up on top of her head in some semblance of a bun, and her face is free from makeup.

"I hope I'm dressed okay?"

It came out as a question, and I see the flecks of self-doubt cross her face. I had seen the same look a few times over the short time I've known her. We had briefly talked about her past relationships when we ate at Dina's Diner, and I couldn't help but feel like her self-doubt was due to the assholes that considered themselves good enough for her. I immediately hate them all.

I reach over to place my hand lightly on her thigh. "You look perfect, Mina."

Her face relaxes as she playfully continues, "And are you going to tell me where it is that you're taking me?"

I laugh, a low rumbling sound that reverberates through the cab of the truck. "Nope."

She scowls, and I can't help but continue to laugh at how adorable the mock pout on her face looks.

I turn on the radio which is set to a country station.

I'm about to ask her if she minds the music, but before I can, she reaches forward and turns the volume up when a Brad Paisley song begins to play. As we drive, we talk about music, and I am surprised to find that her taste in music is as wide as mine. I like a variety of genres, though at first glance, most people wouldn't consider me a country music fan. Mina and I find commonality in that as we talk about various shows and musical festivals we had either attended or hoped to attend one day.

About an hour passes before we turn off the road into the parking area of Morrow Mountain State Park. Getting out of the truck, I come around to help her down. She looks around before stretching her arms up above her head.

Suddenly, I find myself slightly hesitant with the plans I made for us. "When I first met you on the plane, you mentioned one of your favorite parts about living in Portland was the outdoors - the hiking and trails." I shrug as I continue, "I'm sure it's hard to be away, and you're probably missing it. I thought maybe this could help."

She looks surprised, but then reaches out, cupping my cheek in her hand and running her thumb over my skin while her eyes search mine. "This might just be the most thoughtful thing anyone has ever done for me."

"Be careful; you might not be saying that in about five miles."

Her laugh cuts right through me.

She stores her small purse in the glovebox. I pull my backpack and two large bottles of cold water from a cooler in the bed of my truck before handing one to her. I offer her sunscreen which she takes, rubbing it slowly into the designs that coat her skin. She uses a small dollop and swipes it under her eyes, across the bridge of her nose, and around her forehead.

"You missed a spot," I say, reaching out to rub away a small, white streak that was across her cheek. She blushes, and fuck me, it's the sexiest thing I've ever seen.

With my hand on her lower back, I lead her towards the trailhead while musing that something as simple as taking her interests into consideration was her idea of someone treating her well. It shouldn't surprise me. Hell, I used to be one of those men that had a one track mind when it came to women. I wanted them in my bed, and that was the extent of my feelings towards them. As I grew older though, I started to see just how fucking amazing women could be for more than just their bodies.

While most of the other people we pass in the parking lot are headed to the right, we swing to the left. Being one of my favorite places to hike in our area, I know we will get a gorgeous water view for about the last half mile of our hike if we take the trail in this direction. This is a popular trail, and while there are many other less populous places we could have gone, I wanted her to feel safe with me, especially outside of her home and away from her family.

The trails are mostly flat, and while not well marked, I have been exploring them since I was a boy and know my way safely around. Several times, we cross paths with groups of others, politely nodding at them as we walk the mixture of gravel and dirt. Mina is walking next to me when she suddenly trips over a stray rock. Without thinking, I reach out, pulling her into my arms to keep her from falling. That familiar adorable, sexy blush spreads across her cheeks as she quietly thanks me. I hold her just a second longer than necessary before releasing her as I relish in the feel of her body against mine.

While it is warm, the tree coverage provides enough shade that the heat isn't oppressive. Nonetheless, around halfway through the trail, I notice a small trickle of sweat that has trailed down Mina's back, leaving a path of moisture that is visible through her shirt.

We walk several steps off the path, and I guide her to sit on an overturned tree before taking a seat next to her. She downs half her water before running the cool bottle over her neck. We are in the middle of the woods, and watching the tiny drops of condensation fall on her skin has me feeling almost primal. This woman has a way about her that tears me between wanting to be her prince charming while also wanting to claim her like Tarzan of the fucking jungle. Clearing my throat as a way to center myself, I dig into the backpack and pull out two slices of Dina's Diner pie before handing her one.

"You've already found my weakness, I see."

I give her a wink as I laugh, and we clink our plastic forks together in a mock toast before each digging into our respective pie pieces: peanut butter for her, apple for me.

We grow quiet as we eat and watch two small deer nearby. Mina removes her phone from a pocket on the thigh of her yoga pants and snaps a few pictures before they scurry off, frightened by the sound of approaching footsteps. Collecting our trash I place it back into my backpack before helping Mina down from the log we have been sitting on. She steadies herself, her palms against my chest, lips inches from mine.

Before I can make a move, she pushes off of me and spins around so her back is facing mine. "Can we take a picture?" she asks before pulling her phone from the small pocket again. She moves backwards, her back flush against my chest, and I instinctively pull her closer, my arms wrapping around her waist before bringing my head close to hers. She snaps a picture and before she puts her phone away I ask her to take one more. This time, right before she snaps the picture, I turn my face and press a kiss to her temple. A small, almost inaudible gasp escapes her lips.

She slowly turns towards me, her green eyes sparkling. Lips moving to speak, I quiet her before she has the chance, slanting my lips over hers. Mina hesitates for only a moment before leaning into the kiss. She tastes like peanut butter pie and salt, no doubt from the sweat of our hike. As my lips part, she follows suit, allowing my tongue to rove over hers. I nip at her lower lip while pushing her back against a tree. Her hands slide up my chest while I hold her posessively by the back of her neck with one hand, the other lightly teasing the underside of her tank.

Jumping back at the sound of footsteps, she puts space between us right as a family comes down the trail. Nodding to the adults, I glance at Mina to see the cutest, pink blush creeping up her cheeks again. She blushes so easily, and every time she does, I am even more attracted to her. She's so fucking cute.

"We should probably get going," she notes as she heads back to the path, hands wringing together in front of her as if she were ashamed of our actions. I want to protest - to tell her that we should stay right where we are, lips eternally locked together, and my hands endlessly roaming her body. Instead, I hesitantly follow behind Mina.

Our hike continues mostly in silence for about a mile, Mina stopping occasionally to take pictures of the nature around us, me stopping to take mental snapshots of Mina. I can't help but study her as she studies the scenery. Gentle rays of sun pour through the canopy of trees, highlighting her flawless skin. Her hair has started to fall from her bun and I want to pull the elastic free, allowing the rest of the strands to fall around her face.

We continue to hike, and as we come around a bend in the trail, the Yadkin River comes into view, stopping her in her tracks. Her eyes take in the sight of the gentle, rolling river, the rocky shores, children running up and down in the grass nearby, and the men and women fishing along the banks.

"It's beautiful," she almost whispers.

"It is," I reply. But I'm not looking at the river.

She unexpectedly reaches for my hand and pulls me down towards the shore. "Can we put our feet in for a little while?" She sounds excited, almost childlike with her request.

Nodding, I follow her down, stripping my shoes and

socks from my feet. The water is cool and refreshing as I sit next to her on a large rock. "I'm sorry about what happened before."

Catching me off guard, she replies, shaking her head and simply saying, "I'm not."

She takes my hand in her own before leaning her head on my shoulder. "I'm just scared, Nico."

"I know," I reply. "I am, too."

She looked at me quizzically as I continue, unsure of where this sudden burst of vulnerability came from. "I was married before. She wasn't a good wife, and in return, I wasn't a good husband to her, not that it is any excuse. She found comfort with drugs; I found it with other women - almost any woman who would have me."

Mina's body stiffens against me, loosening her grip on my hand. I continue, "We were married right out of highschool and only stayed married for three years. I've grown since then. Hell, I have a therapist."

At that, she laughs, and I retaliate by reaching into the river and flicking water towards her.

Since we enjoyed our day at such a leisurely pace, our short hike had taken much of the afternoon. Knowing we still have about a half mile back to the car as well as an hour ride before us, I urge her to her feet and we both place our socks and shoes back on.

"Why does your brother call you Philly if your name

is Mina?" The question has been bothering me since I first heard Colin use the name.

A groan crosses her lips. "My entire family calls me Philly. They have ever since I was a child. It's short for Philomena, my real name. I hate both Philly and Philomena. Use either, and I'll castrate you."

I laugh, and she continues, "I take it Nico is short for Nicolas?"

I explain to her that she is correct and that I use Nicolas for when I meet with clients who are looking to tour houses for sale. For some reason, even though her brother and I had been friends for several years now, he still insisted on using Nicolas.

Returning to the truck, I grab two full bottles of water from the cooler, handing one to Mina before downing my own. I hold out my hand to her and she graciously accepts it as she climbs back into the truck.

We chat casually most of the way back to her house while the sun slowly sets outside the truck windows. We talk more about music, how she wants to do some sketches based on the pictures she took today, and how she is excited to start tattooing again this coming week. She already has people emailing for appointments and was confident she would be working more than two days a week soon. She was surprised to learn that many of my tattoos came from Broken Sparrow, and she laughed when I told her that if she was nice, maybe I'd let her do my next piece.

Scrolling through the pictures she took during the day while I continue to drive, she swings the phone towards me to show me the one we took together. Though I only glance quickly, sure to keep my eyes on the road, what I could see was nothing short of magnificent.

"Let me see the next one," I playfully chide.

Swiping to the next picture, the one where I playfully kissed her, she turns the phone to me once again. Her eyes were closed in the picture, an adorable crinkle of laugh lines on the outer edge of each eye. Her lips were pressed together, but not in a hard line. Instead, they curled into the most beautiful smile I had ever seen.

"Send them to me?"

"Only if I can post them to my Instagram."

"Only if you tag me in them," I reply

She nods at me as her fingers fly across her phone screen. A moment later, I hear my phone ding in my pocket.

Joking with her, I tell her not to go sending them to all her friends back in Portland because they'd certainly be jealous of her.

Laughing with Mina is easy. She responds by

saying she wouldn't dare, only hesitating a minute before sending them to her best friend. I, of course, am curious to know if I will pass whatever the best friend test was between the two women and was hopeful it was good when Mina read something from her phone screen a short time later before bursting into a fit of laughter.

"She says if you're too much trouble for me, that she'll take you off my hands."

Smirking at her, I playfully respond, "Mina, I plan on being just enough trouble for you."

She bites her lip and turns her head back to her phone.

We pull up in front of her brother's house a short while later, and I reluctantly open the truck door for her, not wanting our day to be over. Hugging her, I ask her the question that has been on my mind since the second I saw her that morning. "When can I see you again?"

"Nico," she says my name about an octave lower than her normal tone.

I interrupt her. "I don't like the sound of that."

Continuing, she says, "I do want to see you again. But please," she pauses, "know that I need to move slowly."

I nod, swinging my chin towards the front porch.

"I'd kiss you goodnight, but it appears we have an audience."

She follows my gaze to the windows off the porch and laughs when she sees her two nieces with their faces all but plastered against the glass pane. Waving them away, she waits until their faces have vanished before pressing her lips to mine in a chaste kiss.

As she moves to walk towards the door, I grab her wrist at the last second, pulling her back against me. I envelope her in my arms, tipping her chin back to meet my lips. She grins into my kiss as I run my hands down her heavily tattooed arms.

Before releasing her from my embrace, I lean down to her ear.

"As slow as you need, baby. As slow as you need."

She lets herself inside as I return to my truck, sliding behind the wheel and placing the keys in the ignition. Before driving away, I take my phone from my pocket and open up my neglected Instagram account. Notifications light up in the upper right hand corner or the app, and I click on them, smiling when I see I have been tagged in a post and have a new follower. Clicking the notification, mine and Mina's smiling faces fill my screen. I swipe across the picture to see she has attached the second picture we took as well: the one of me kissing her temple. The caption is simple, but it makes me laugh when I recognize the Nicki Minaj lyrics .

Mina_Inks: "I said, 'Excuse me, @NicoSells a hell of a guy."

I take a minute to scroll through the comments that have flooded the post. At least her followers seem to think we'd be good together, even if she still seems apprehensive.

I shoot her a text, not caring that it's only been a few minutes since we parted.

Me: *Really? Super Bass?*

She texts back immediately, a simple shrug emoji.

I drive away from her brother's house, a huge smile plastered on my face, and Super Bass blasting from Spotify like I'm a teenage girl who just got her license.

Seven
MINA

It had only been a few weeks since I returned to Johnson Creek, but already, I had settled into a nice routine. Each Tuesday and Thursday, I would make my way to Broken Sparrow, happy that my books were already filled with appointments. Between clients, I spent time helping Raven around the studio and slowly began to forge relationships with the other three artists as well.

Most adults that I knew liked their jobs, but I felt lucky to be one of the few that actually loved what they did for a living. Talking to a potential client, putting their ideas onto paper, turning that into artwork on skin—I truly loved every part of the process.

The bell above the door chimes, and I look towards the small lobby to see Steph enter the shop. We had continued to chat since I came back to Johnson Creek and I was excited that she wanted to honor her grandmother, the infamous Dina in which Dina's Diner was named after, with a particularly fitting tattoo.

While I was proficient in many types of artwork, I preferred to work in what many in my industry would consider a neo-traditional style. I loved bold lines, saturated colors, and an illustrative look that pulled from nature. Steph had given me creative liberties with what would be permanently inked on her skin, and while I kept some of my signature style in her art, it also showed her fun and free spirited personality while paying tribute to her late grandmother.

With Steph sitting in my chair, I open my sketch pad to the drawing I had been working on, and as soon as her eyes take in the design, she squeals.

"It. Is. Perfect," she punctuates each word in her signature excited pitch and adds a little lilt to the last word.

A mug of coffee sits in the background of the drawing, steam rising from it into swirls that create a heart. The foreground has a giant piece of apple pie topped with an oversized dollop of whipped cream. Of course, I would have personally preferred it to be peanut butter pie, but as with all my clients, this tattoo wasn't for me.

After I place the stencil on her shoulder blade and Steph approves its placement, we proceed with the outline before moving into color - my favorite part of any tattoo. Dipping into various inks, my design comes alive on her skin in hues of browns, greens, purples and blues. While I work, she alternates between chatting with me and listening to music through her headphones, trying her best to find a small semblance of zen amongst the pain of being under my needles.

Steph and I had grown up together, living only a few blocks away in our small town. As children, we often played together, spending our summer days swimming at the local lake or sitting at the old school soda fountain bar in the diner eating her grandmother's famous pies. In high school, we were both considered outsiders, more concerned with art and theater than studying and boys. We drifted apart when I left for art school and she stayed in Johnson Creek to help run the diner after her grandmother passed. We had been spending time together since I came home, and it truly had been great to reconnect with an old friend.

But damn was she a squirmy bitch in my chair.

Just as we are nearing the end of Steph's tattoo,

Colin walks in, my nieces close behind. He hasn't been keen on promising the girls that he would bring them to see what it was like to get a tattoo in person, but after endless hours of the girls begging to come to Broken Sparrow, he finally relented.

The girls were reluctant to get too close, but I assured them it was safe and that it was okay for them to come to my workstation. Like two wide-eyed does, they tentatively step closer as I work the last strokes of ink into the design. Emily, being younger and more reserved, is more content to stay close to her father while Laurel eagerly stands next to me.

Watching as I wipe away stray ink and blood on the skin before wrapping Steph's tattoo, Laurel asks questions both to me about how I worked and to Steph about how much the tattoo hurt.

Before heading home, Colin says he is going to take the girls to dinner. Steph is my last client of the day, and my nieces have tons of questions, so we decide to join them. My family leaves, and we are shortly behind after I finish cleaning my work station, being sure everything is properly sanitized for the evening.

We chat on the short walk to the Italian restaurant, another Johnson Creek business that has withstood the test of time and corporate takeovers. That was one of the things I most loved about my hometown. No matter how much time passed, we still supported our local businesses and wanted to see them thrive.

Steph holds the door open for me when we enter the small restaurant, and I quickly scan the space for my brother, ready to shove my face full of delicious garlic knots and fresh pasta as the smell of garlic permeates the air. Instead of Colin, I find a familiar pair of deep, brown eyes that heat when they lock with mine.

Nico.

We have talked several times since the day he took me on that beautiful hike a few weeks ago. I was impressed that he actually remembered our small talk on the plane and had planned a day around something that was important to me. He kissed me like he couldn't get enough of my lips, and honestly, it heated me to my core. Still, I was reluctant to move forward with Nico. Part of me was afraid of a relationship with him. No matter how slow he offered to take it, he would strain his relationship with Colin and I could very well do the same if things didn't work out. I still didn't know much about his past, and it didn't bother me that he was previously married, but it did bother me that he had a difficult relationship with his ex. I wanted someone who would love me, who deserved me. Could that be Nico?

I approach the table, and he stands, coming towards

me and taking me in a tender embrace, kissing my cheek before releasing me while my nieces giggle behind us. Two open seats at the table remain, one between my nieces and one next to Nico. My nieces promptly pull Steph between them, asking her how her shoulder blade felt and when they could see her tattoo again, leaving me to take the seat next to Nico.

I quickly down a glass of the house white wine before ordering a second, popping a garlic knot smothered in Alfredo sauce into my mouth while I wait for our server to return. From the corner of my eye, I can see Nico slowly studying me, and I'm not sure if it is how hungry I am from not eating or if the wine had already loosened my nerves around him, but I dart my tongue out and run it along my bottom lip, lapping up some stray sauce that had made its way to the small corner of my mouth. In response, his hand leaves the table and settles on my thigh, his fingers slowly drawing circles on the exposed skin beneath the hem of my shorts.

My breath hitches, and my head swirls.

"What do you think, Mina?" Steph's voice snaps me back to the present.

"I'm sorry." I quickly try to bring myself back to the table, Nico's hand still sitting on my thigh, dangerously close to the hem of my shorts. "I must have zoned out."

She laughs incredulously and shoots me a playful

look before continuing, "Saturday night, a bunch of us are going to The Living Room for karaoke. Please say you'll come with us? Bring your friends from work. The guys already said they were in!"

The mention of the name makes me laugh. A hot spot halfway between Johnson Creek and Charlotte, The Living Room is not an actual living room but is a bar known for craft beers, signature drinks, and live entertainment. Oversized couches and recliners flank the bar, most drinks are served in a mishmash of old, snarky coffee mugs, and they have hundreds of board games and puzzles you can bring to your coffee table to play. I spent many nights there, way underage, playing games, singing karaoke, and drinking way more than I should have. It had been years since I thought of the place, and it conjures up memories that have me smiling.

After some gentle teasing from my brother, Steph, and Nico, I agree to go with one condition.

"I am *not* singing."

Steph loudly laughs, receiving the looks of several other patrons in the restaurant "Yeah, right, Mina. You say that now."

I did like to sing. I had been told I had a nice voice. In my old life - my Portland life - I would often frequent bars with Daphne on karaoke night. We would croon silly songs together. The Spice Girls were our go-to. We were never serious when we got up on stage together, but whatever we did, it certainly helped us to score free drinks.

Our table continues to talk while we eat, Colin and Nico reliving memories of house hunting with Tabitha, the girls laughing at stories of their mom. It saddens me to not have my sister-in-law here with us in the flesh, saddens me that we never became as close as we should have, but it also makes my heart swell to hear the stories and memories of her and to see how her family - my family - is keeping her memory alive.

We finish our meal, Colin graciously refusing to accept money from any of us at the table, and then, we make our way towards the exit. Nico, behind me, slowly leads me with his hand on my lower back. His touch sizzles through my thin shirt, setting my skin ablaze.

The girls run ahead to Colin's car while the four of us adults say our goodnights, Nico again cradling me in a soul-awakening embrace.

"Saturday," he says, more a command than a question.

Slowly, I nod "Saturday," I agree, the words coming out barely a whisper.

His hand cups the side of my face, and I melt into

his touch before he turns and walks towards his truck that is parked across the street.

I watch him climb into his truck and listen to the engine come alive before repeating the word again, more to myself than anyone else, as I hurry my pace to catch up with my brother and friend.

Eight

Nico

It has been less than 48 hours since I saw Mina, but that woman has me acting like a lovesick teenager. I had long since put my hard partying ways behind me, trading in late nights at the bar picking up women for long hours both at work and working on the house I was renovating. But knowing she was going to be there tonight, I had jumped at the chance to go.

I spend the better part of Saturday tearing carpet from the downstairs of the early 1900s Victorian just outside of Charlotte that I had purchased in March. The house had been used most recently as a bed and breakfast before sitting vacant for several years, the previous owners gutting it from almost all of the original features. Aside from some original stained glass over the front door, most of the house was unable to be salvaged.

It was a damn shame.

I wasn't exactly in the market for an almost 3,000 square foot home that needed a total remodel when I first came across the house. I had been helping a couple to find a home in the same neighborhood and something kept bringing me back to its front door. It sat on just under three acres, almost unheard of in this area, and backed up to a small creek.

The lawn was overgrown and full of weeds. The entire house, while livable, needed major improvements to turn it back into a single-family dwelling, and it seemed to creak and moan with the slightest of breeze. It most definitely was one hundred percent haunted.

Sweat dripping down my back, I sling the last roll of carpet into the rented dumpster in the driveway. Layers of muck and glue dot the now uncarpeted floors, but I am still hopeful to find the original hardwood flooring under the layers of grime.

Climbing the stairs to the second story, I peel my shirt off before entering the one working bathroom the house currently has. Kicking out of my shorts and boxer briefs, I flip the water on, and it spurts to life over God-awful, blue-tiled shower walls. I step under the stream of cool water, erasing the day's sweat and grime from my body.

My mind, as it so frequently does these days, strays to Mina, and inadvertently, my hand moves to my dick which is unsurprisingly already hard. I can't stop thinking of her pouty lips, how she licked alfredo sauce off them, and how she bit that bottom lip of hers when she was deep in concentration.

Of course, that only leads me to think of those same lips wrapped around my cock-lust filled eyes looking up at me while she sucked me off.

I increase the tempo of my hand, lathered and tugging my cock, while I brace myself against the shower wall.

And then, I think about Mina again.

I think about her on her knees with tears leaking from those perfect, catlike eyes as my cock throbs against the back of her throat, mascara running down her cheeks as she swallows my cum. I think about her on her back, legs spread wide as she lets me worship what is sure to be an absolutely perfectly tight little pussy with my tongue. I think about sliding my cock into her cunt, and her ass, and between those tits. My God, those perfect tits.

And just like that, surrounded by tile, now frigid,

cold water, and my own grunts, I shudder and in hard spurts paint the tile wall with ropes of my cum.

I clean both myself and the shower wall and then pull on a dark pair of jeans with a white t-shirt. Generally, I don't pay too much attention to what I wear, but Mina and I had a few conversations about our respective tattoos, and I know she appreciates when mine are on display. Of course, I feel the same about hers.

Pulling into the back row of the parking lot at The Living Room, I walk with purpose into the bar, solely set on finding my girl as quickly as possible. The air inside the bar assaults my senses as soon as the door opens, smelling like sticky spillage of stale beer, sweat, and oppressive cologne from overly optimistic men hoping to score. It is disgusting and oddly familiar at the same time.

I quickly scan the room, my eyes meeting Mina's as she sucks a drink through a straw tucked into a mug. As I walk toward her, she places her drink on the coffee table in front of her and stands to meet me. I pull her in for a hug, lingering a bit longer than necessary as the smells of the dingy bar are fully replaced with the aroma of sandalwood and fresh linen.

Her scent causes my dick to twitch, and I pull back before I end up fully erect in the middle of the bar. I shake Colin's hand, and he pulls me in to slap me on the back, making me even more glad that I had pulled back from Mina when I did. The last thing I needed was to have a fucking hard on when in such close proximity to my best friend, who just so happens to be Mina's fucking brother.

"Don't fuck this up."

His words catch me off guard and when I pull back, he juts his chin in the direction of his sister as if silently giving his approval. This isn't the first time he has given me this approval, and I grin, nodding back at him.

Grabbing a beer from the bucket that had been delivered to our table, I return to Mina, perching myself on the arm of the oversized chair she sits on as she thumbs through a book of karaoke songs. Steph joins us along with a few others from the diner and Mina's job, and we all settle in, me staying close to Mina. Having several other men in our group that I am unfamiliar with has my guard up, and I feel overly protective of the woman next to me who has infiltrated my mind.

While she looks gorgeous every day, by night, she takes on an entirely new look - a total vixen. Her hair cascades down in waves, her pink hair down to the middle of her back. A dark, denim-mini skirt looks like it was painted to her curves, and a black corset is clasped up her front, putting her ample cleavage on full display. Her eyes...damn, those eyes. They are outlined in thick kohl that flicks out on the edges, making them appear even more cat-like in appearance. Her lips are a glossy deep violet, and my mind drifts to what the color would look like marking my cock. She wears a thin, black choker around her neck, several bangles on each wrist, and the biggest hoop earrings I have ever seen.

She excuses herself to get another drink, and reluctantly, I watch as she saunters to the bar. As expected, every damn head in that place turns as she walks by. She really has no idea how fucking beautiful she is.

I take the opportunity to gesture Colin over to me. My tone still low, I ask, "you're okay with this?"

He hesitates a moment before responding.

"I can tell she likes you, and clearly, you seem to have a thing for her. She's a good woman. Just- don't fuck her over, Nicolas."

A smile spreads across my face as I nod to my friend.

Several minutes have passed, and Mina still hasn't returned. Feeling anxious without her next to me, I turn to find her at the bar. A man I don't know is way too close to her, eyeing her greedily. I don't want to interfere; I know she can handle herself, but when I lock eyes with her, I can see her silently pleading for some interference.

I take long strides across the bar, coming up next to her just as the man tries to reach out to touch her waist. Putting myself between the two, my arm instinctively curls around the base of her neck in a possessive hold. I want to punch this fucker in the face, want to rearrange his features until he is unrecognizable. Instead of turning to violence, I stake my claim on Mina by turning her towards me and pulling her lips to mine, kissing her deep while keeping eye contact with this fucking asshole who thought he could touch what was mine.

"Nico." Her voice is breathy and barely a whisper above the sound of the bar.

As the man stomps away, I reach up and cup her face while leaning down to her ear to speak over the person absolutely butchering Dave Matthews Band. "You're safe with me, Mina. At some point, you'll start believing me when I tell you that."

I trail my thumb from her bottom lip and trace down her throat before dropping my hand to take hers in mine. Her breathing has become labored, her eyes slightly hooded. I don't know if it is from the alcohol she's been drinking or from me. I hope it's the latter of the two.

We rejoin the rest of our friends, her hand in mine the entire time. Cards Against Humanity is being played on the coffee table when we return. Colin is actually laughing at something someone said, and several of the girls are loudly singing along to the next performer on stage.

Someone in our group orders a round of shots, and as a server delivers them, the emcee comes over the mic, his voice loudly booming and commanding the room. "Friends, please welcome our next performer to the stage, Mina!"

Her eyes widen before she turns to Steph while shaking her head, "Oh no, no, no, no, no!"

Steph quickly responds with "Oh yes, yes, yes, yes, yes!"

Long seconds pass between the two friends locked in a stalemate before Mina slowly stands, tosses back both her shot and mine, and plods to the stage.

As she climbs onto the small platform The Living Room calls a stage, Beggin' by Måneskin begins to fill the room. Without hesitation, she launches into the song while turning to Steph, playfully flipping her friend off.

Fuck, my girl could sing. Sure, we had playfully sung along to a few songs in my truck when we drove home from our hike, but now, she wasn't being playful. She was singing and unloading her soul onto the audience as she did, and of course, every eye in the entire bar was locked on her.

Like a magnet pulling me towards her, I stand and stride to the front of the small stage, my beer still in hand. One hand on the mic, the other roves her body as she sings, her eyes locked on mine as she sways her hips on stage like I am the only person in the entire bar.

I shift my weight, hoping to hide the growing bulge pressed dangerously tight against my zipper.

As the last line of the song is sung, she replaces the mic in its stand, oblivious to the way the crowd in the bar cheers for her. Her eyes are still on mine as she steps down, placing her hand on my arm to steady herself as she descends the few stairs that lead from the stage. I am suddenly more overcome with need for this woman than for the air filling my own lungs.

I practically pull her through the bar and towards the door, only stopping to drop my still half-full bottle of beer on the bartop. Her small, stiletto-clad feet work overtime to keep up with my long strides. My body takes control, my mind barely having time to catch up before I have her outside, around the side of the building, and pressed against the brick exterior.

My lips hungrily find hers, my hands winding through her hair, and as I run my tongue over her lips, I press myself against her body. She responds with a gasp.

"Fuck, Mina. Tell me right now you don't feel something between us. Tell me right now to stop, and I will. But so help me, God, if you don't tell me to stop..."

She cuts me off before I can finish, pulling me back

to her mouth to greedily kiss me. Her tongue delves into my mouth, licking and sucking, taking what's hers. Her hands are against my chest, and I swear, my dick gets even harder in response to her touch.

"I don't want to move slow anymore, Nico."

Not even bothering to look to see if anyone is around, I cup her breasts through her tight corset, needing to feel her under my hands. She groans into my mouth, spurring me on. I slide my hand down her stomach as I thrust my leg between her thighs to push her legs further apart. Eagerly, I bunch her skirt around her waist until there is nothing but lace between her pussy and my hand. Sliding the fabric to the side, I slowly dip my finger into her slick folds. Damn, she is fucking drenched.

I meticulously work my fingers over her clit, rubbing her in slow circles as she grinds herself against me further, heat flashing in her eyes.

She nearly pants, her head dropping back "Nico - God, Nico, I need more."

At her words, I slide two fingers into her pussy, feeling the walls of her core clenching around my fingers, begging for more. Fuck, she is tight. My pace quickens, and I am surprised when she asks me to go harder. My beautiful angel likes it rough, and I'm not one to disappoint.

I insert one more digit into her soaking cunt and furiously finger fuck her, her back still against the brick. I am unrelentless as her breathing quickens, her eyes locking with mine.

I know the moment she comes, her pussy walls clenching tight around my fingers, her body shuttering against mine, her legs almost giving out as I keep her pinned to the wall. She rides out her orgasm, my fingers still inside of her, and I feel her wetness trickle down my hand to my wrist.

I inch my fingers from inside her, and while still holding her eyes, bring my fingers to her lips, hoping she doesn't hesitate. Again, she surprises me, eagerly lapping her own wetness from my fingers until they are clean.

I'm pretty sure I feel lightheaded as all the blood in my body rushes to my cock, and it presses painfully hard against my zipper.

I drop my head to hers, taking her mouth with mine, desperate to taste her on her own mouth. I lightly trace her bottom lip with my tongue before slanting both of my lips over hers. She tastes so fucking sweet, like her desire mixed with whatever fruity drink she had been drinking throughout the night.

She pulls back from our kiss, and I feel the loss of her heat immediately. I brace myself for her to speak, knowing that if she walks away from me right now that I would never recover. Instead, the sweetest words escape her kiss swollen lips.

"Take me home with you, Nico."

Nine

MINA

As soon as the words leave my mouth, Nico drops his forehead to mine, a wicked glint in his eyes. His lips come crashing to mine again, and I taste the beer on his tongue. I'm hungry for him - starved. But this time, he cuts our kiss short.

Before I know what is happening, he pulls me from where I am still pushed against the wall, bends down, picks me up, and tosses me over his shoulder. I start to protest, but a firm hand lands on my denim-clad ass with an audible thwack, causing me to gasp before leaving me speechless.

I was beyond pissed at Steph for signing me up to sing tonight and was still annoyed when I took the stage, but the second I saw Nico looking at me on that stage, any anger I had left my body. I might have been the one on display for the entire bar to see, but still, he tracked my every move with wanting eyes. I felt like prey beneath his gaze. I suddenly wanted to perform just for him.

So, I did.

Keeping my gaze locked on him, I teased him, slowly running my hands up and down my body. I tossed my long curls about and slowly licked my lips between lines of the song.

Clearly, it had an effect on him. And now, he was eagerly stalking towards his truck in long, hurried strides with me over his shoulder. His palm runs dangerously up the side of my thigh, and after finger fucking me against the side of the bar just minutes before, I already want him again.

When we reach the truck, he sets me down on my feet gently, tucking a few stray hairs behind my ear before speaking gruffly, his voice laced with want. "I'm not sure how I'm going to be able to keep my hands off of you for the drive back to my place when all I want to do is strip you down bare and have my way with you. Right now. Right here."

My breath hitches as a familiar pool of electric energy starts in my stomach and quickly spreads further south. The dichotomy between his two sides confuses me - the gentle Nico who wants to care for me and set me down cautiously, and the dark alter-ego who is this extremely ravenous sexual being who needed to take me against a building in public.

I want both of his sides.

I want *him*.

As if I am speaking my thoughts out loud, he continues, "But, I'm not going to do that to you. Not tonight. You deserve more than that. Tonight, I'm going to take you home. I'm going to kiss and lick every fucking inch of your body. And only after I've explored every secret your body holds, only then, am I going to take you with my dick."

He takes my mouth with his again, and I swear every time he does, he possesses just a bit more of my soul. When we break apart, he reaches around me to open the door before helping me climb into the cab of the truck. Closing the door, he walks around the front of the truck, quickly taking out his phone and messing with it for a minute before he climbs into the driver's side.

The truck engine revs to life, and Chris Stapleton's gentle voice croons on the radio, singing about wanting to stay but knowing he should probably leave.

Nico throws his phone to the dash.

"I asked Colin to take your purse home for you."

Shit. I was so preoccupied with what was happening

between Nico and myself that I didn't even think about my purse. Suddenly aware of what he just said, knowing that my brother knows what I am about to do with his best friend, doubt creeps in again, and I feel the sudden urge to flee the truck. Nico reaches out for my wrist, firmly clasping it.

"Hey, look at me."

I comply, slowly turning my head to meet his eyes - his incredibly sexy, honey-molten eyes.

Some people might think that brown eyes are over-rated, but not me – not his, not his brown eyes that sear through my soul and are full of mystery, not his brown eyes that conjure up images of wood grained mahogany

He continues while rubbing circles on my wrist with his strong fingers. "Stop overthinking things. We don't have to do this, Mina. Do you want to go back inside the bar?"

I shake my head

"Do you trust me?" he asks.

I nod.

And with that nod, he pulls the truck from its parking spot, and we drive towards the unknown.

We make the short drive to Nico's house with only the music from the radio breaking the silence between us. His fingers stay linked with mine the entire time, and when we approach his house, he gives my hand a small squeeze before releasing it to safely maneuver us into the small driveway.

His house is beautiful, albeit in need of some TLC. Steep gabled roofs meld with circular angles. Large bay windows flank either side of the front door. There are several turrets and dormers, and as we walk towards the door, I see beautiful stained glass above it.

"Wow." The word comes out breathy. "This place is..."

Nico laughs before finishing my sentence, "a mess."

"No, it's stunning. Really."

We enter the house, and I quickly notice the state of disarray. The floors are rough and uneven, the walls are covered in spackle and what I assume are paint samples, and a room to the left holds a ton of unpacked boxes.

"I told you; it's a mess."

My head moves side to side as if I'm contemplating his words. "More like a work in progress. I can see what you saw in this place. It's going to be spectacular when you finish it."

"Yeah," Nico responds, "if I ever get it finished."

He leads me upstairs, cautioning me to watch my step on the steep incline. Tools are scattered throughout the hallway, and he inadvertently kicks a hammer as he leads me to the bedroom, mumbling a curse under his breath.

"I only have one room and bathroom that are livable right now." He almost sounds nervous when he says it, like he is worried I'm going to judge his living situation.

Hoping to lighten the mood, I turn to look at him as we enter the small room he has set up with minimal furniture, "so, Nico, you're telling me you don't bring lots of women here?"

My words seem to have the opposite of the intended effect. He tenses and his eyes go dark before he speaks, his voice deep and gravelly. "I haven't wanted to bring anyone here since the day I met you, Mina."

Nico always seems so strong on the exterior. This glimpse into his vulnerable side causes butterflies to flutter throughout my chest. I close the small gap between us, lightly covering his lips with mine.

He deepens the kiss, my mouth opening beneath his. My hands slowly slide down his muscular chest until my fingers play with the hem of his shirt. Breaking apart, I lift his shirt over his head and gasp when I see him shirtless for the first time.

The man is a fucking Greek God. His broad chest tapers to a slim waist, an honest to goodness fucking sixpack on display, and a gorgeously sexy deep vee leading to the holy grail that resides below his belt. For the first time, I can really study his tattoos. His right arm is covered in a sprawling underwater scene that stretches from his wrist to his shoulder. A giant octopus perches atop his shoulder, its tentacles spreading out across his chest. On his left, the same amount of ink covers him, but instead of the ocean, it's of the sky. Birds in flight trickle up his arm into the clouds and fade into a galaxy of stars and planets.

As if two opposite poles of magnets, my hands instinctively reach out to his skin and lightly trace the designs permanently placed on his body. I trail my fingers up his arms and across his chest before moving myself to his back.

Sky and water crash together on his strong back. An intricately detailed shipwreck covers most of the space. Sun beams cut through the water from the left while a menacing shark swims underneath, appearing to disappear under the band of his pants.

It's intense and chaotic and beautiful and breathtaking all at once. The emotion of seeing such beautiful work swirls inside my chest, and suddenly, I feel unanticipated tears prick behind my eyelids.

"You're beautiful, Nico," I all but whisper.

He turns to face me with a new intensity in his gaze. Painstaking slow, his strong hands come to meet the delicate satin fabric of my corset. He pushes my hair back behind my shoulders and trails his fingers over my collarbone, sending shivers down my spine.

Eyes still locked with mine, he releases the clasps that run down the front of the corset. The material slowly falls away from my body. As he unhooks the last clasp, it falls completely away, landing on the ground around us and leaving me bare chested before the hungriest eyes I have ever seen.

Impulsively, I go to shield myself with my arm, but Nico stops me.

"Don't hide from me, Mina."

I shudder as he brings his hand up to my face, cupping my cheek with his large hand. He slides it down the side of my neck, over my collarbone once again, before continuing to lower his hand to my breasts. He traces the sternum tattoo that rests under my chest, a delicate lace and jewel like piece. He slides his fingers, callused from hours of work on his house, over one nipple, feather light at first then harder, turning it into a tight little bundle of nerve endings. Repeating the process with my other breast, I step into his touch and slide my arms around his neck before moving my hands up against the short hair that covers his scalp with just enough growth on top to tug on. As I slide my hands back down to his chest, I graze my nails against his skin.

"Goddammit, Mina," he hisses through clenched teeth.

Without warning, his arms go around me, and he

lifts me off the ground. My legs wrap around his waist, pushing up my skirt, and for a few glorious seconds as he walks me over to the bed, his hard chest presses up against my bare breasts.

He all but throws me to the bed, and before I even have a chance to bounce on the spring mattress, he is on top of me, ravaging my mouth with his. We're a clash of lips and tongues and teeth.

Nico slides down my body, trailing kisses from my lips down my neck until he comes to my breasts. He swipes his tongue over my right nipple, and a moan slides past my lips. Soft swipes turn into hungry sucking as he presses my tits together. Moving between nipples, he licks and sucks and bites, and when he does, my back arches off the mattress, pressing my tits even closer to his face.

The area between my legs is pulsing and I press my thighs together, desperate to feel the added pressure against my clit. Never - and I mean never - has a man made me almost come from absolutely worshiping my breasts.

But as I'm quickly coming to know, most men aren't Nico.

"More," I rasp. "Nico, I need more."

He moves off my body, and slowly, agonizingly slow, he pulls my bunched up skirt down my legs, discarding it on the floor. All that stands between him and my total nakedness are the lacy black underwear that are already fully coated in my wetness.

Hands on my calves, he pulls me down the bed until my ass sits flush with the edge. He traces over my pussy with one thumb, feeling me through the fabric.

"Fuck, you're wet."

I nod while replying breathlessly, "for you."

A hand on each hip, he moves them to the band of my panties and continues working them down my legs and over my feet. Nico lifts the damp panties to his nose and deeply inhales my scent, his eyes closing as he takes it into his lungs. Somehow, it's the sexiest fucking thing I've ever seen in my life. He tucks my panties into his back pocket before returning his hands to my thighs, spreading them wide.

I'm in this extremely vulnerable position, spread for this absolute Adonis of a man, my juices leaking from myself, and yet, I'm not afraid. I don't feel the immediate need to shield myself. I feel wanted- beautiful even.

His eyes roam my body, fueled by hunger. I can see his cock straining behind the zipper of his jeans, and all I want to do is touch him. I go to move to him, but he stops me, pushing me back to the bed.

"No." It's the only word to escape his lips.

I plead with him using my eyes, but he is undeterred.

"Did you already forget what I said in that parking lot?"

I shake my head.

Then, he is at my feet, taking one leg and propping it up on his shoulder as he runs his fingers up and down my calf. Goosebumps break out across my body as his lips replace his hand.

"Fuck, Mina. You have no idea how long I've been waiting to taste you. The moment I saw you walk through that airport, I knew I needed to have you. When you didn't call that first night - fuck, it killed me."

He releases my leg, and his kisses move towards my center.

If I thought his fingers on my pussy felt good, his mouth on me is absolute heaven. With long, languid strokes, he licks up and down my folds before resting his lips over my clit. He lightly sucks on it before darting his tongue out to run small circles over me, and I swear for a minute, I leave my body.

"So perfect," he murmurs against my skin.

He inserts two long fingers into me while he continues to work my clit with his tongue, licking and lapping and worshiping me. His other hand slides up my body, kneading my breasts.

I arch my hips to press my pussy further into his face while reaching down to run my nails against his scalp. He responds by slipping another finger into my wetness while increasing the urgency of his thrusts.

He pulls away just long enough to pant, "fucking hell, Mina. I could come in my pants just listening to you."

How the hell does he manage to make everything that comes out of his mouth sound so fucking hot?

Continuing to lavish my cunt with his mouth and fingers, I begin to feel the familiar heat of an orgasm build deep in my stomach.

"Nico. Oh...oh, yes!"

"Say it," he growls into my pussy. "Tell me what you want, baby."

I barely hesitate. I have never asked a man for exactly what I want before. I have never enjoyed dirty talk or being more assertive in the bedroom, but with Nico, it all feels natural.

Panting, the words cross my lips as nothing but a husky whisper, "Please, I want to cum."

And holy shit, does he make me cum.

He nips at my clit with his teeth, just grazing it enough to send tingles through my body. He drops his hand from my dripping pussy and grasps my hips, lifting my ass off the bed. He stands, dragging me towards him until my ass is flush with his chest all while keeping his mouth on me. Only my shoulders remain on the bed as I crane my neck to watch him assault me in the very best way possible.

I come apart from the inside out, a guttural sound escaping from deep within my lungs as waves of pleasure course through my body. Nico keeps his mouth on me, unrelenting. I feel myself dripping, my juices leaking from my pussy to run down between my ass and Nico's chest.

I want to be embarrassed that I've made a mess, embarrassed over how wet I am, but as Nico growls his approval into me, I just can't find it in me to care.

He holds me in place for several long moments as the aftershocks of my orgasm roll through my body before lowering me gently back to the mattress. Crawling on the bed next to me, he faces me, taking me into his arms. There is desire in his eyes as his soft lips glide over mine, and I taste myself on his mouth.

I expect him to undress and climb on top of me, but he surprises me when he pushes off the mattress and begins walking away.

"I'll be right back; don't move."

I freeze, insecurity slowly seeping into the cracks he has managed to put in my walls.

He comes back a short while later, a washcloth in

one hand, a few bags of various snacks and two bottles of water in the other.

I'm still unsure upon his return. Worried that suddenly, he didn't want to touch me. "Did...did I do something wrong?"

His eyes snap to mine, and his face softens when he sees what must be doubt spread over my features.

"No, doll. I don't want to rush this." I look at him quizzically as he settles between my legs, using the warm washcloth to clean me before he continues, "It's been weeks, and you're the only fucking thing I can think about. I think about you when I'm awake and dream about you when I'm asleep. I want to devour you, and I fully intend to. But first, let's devour these snacks so you can keep up your strength. You're going to need it."

I laugh as he settles next to me in bed, pulling a blanket over us. He holds out a bottle of water to me, and I graciously take it.

And then, we sit in bed, me still fully naked, him shirtless.

And we eat the snacks.

Ten

Nico

"Tell me about your tattoos," Mina asks, and the question catches me off guard. We're sprawled out in bed in a tangle of sheets, bags of chips, pretzels, and crackers tossed about as she runs her fingers over the tentacles of the octopus that start on my chest and run up to my neck.

I know the ink on my body draws curiosity from most people but few are brave enough to ask about them. I started collecting ink in my early twenties as a way to draw a barrier between myself and the world after my parents died. I used the tattoos as a way to make myself look tough even when I was crumbling on the inside. The high of getting a tattoo is something many people say is addicting, and I can attest to that being absolutely true.

I could lie to Mina, tell her stories about the designs that run over most of my chest, arms, and back, but I don't want to lie to her about this- or anything. So, I tell her the truth.

"Almost everything you've seen, so far, is a tribute to my parents. My dad was obsessed with the sky. He was a pilot and was always looking for a way to get closer to the stars. I swear, if he could, he would have signed up for one of those civilian missions into space. My mom was an ocean lover. We spent our summers at the beach when I was growing up, doing everything from coastal cleanups to helping with marine wildlife rehabilitation. She taught us that it was important to give back to the community instead of just taking all the resources the earth offered to us."

She continues to trail her fingers over my upper body, tracing the designs inked into my skin. "You speak about your parents in the past tense?"

I look at her and nod before continuing. Talking about my parents isn't something I do with people except for my sister and long standing therapist, but Mina isn't just people. "They passed away when I was 19- small plane crash; my dad was the pilot. Every month, we would fly into a different small airport and meet up with other people who flew small planes for breakfast. It's called a fly-in. We would come from all over the state, have breakfast, talk about aviation, then fly home. I loved it as a kid, but as I got older, I found other interests and didn't want to go anymore. The day they died, my sister was at her friend's house, and I was supposed to go but threw a typical, teenage fit, deciding I was too cool to hang out with a bunch of aviation-crazed people. They left late, and the weather turned unexpectedly bad on the flight there."

My voice is slightly hushed as I finish, the emotion and guilt daring to push its way back into my life. Mina cups my face with her hands, and when she looks up to meet my gaze, there are tears in her eyes. "I'm so sorry, Nico," she says, her voice so small and quiet.

I pull her close to me, her exposed body pressed against my naked chest as I place my head on top of hers, deeply taking in her scent. "It was a long time ago."

She leans up to me, kissing me intensely as if she is trying to erase the pain. Slowly sliding her way up my body, she straddles me over my jeans, and any hurt I'm feeling is immediately replaced with the desperate need to be inside her. She slowly circles her hips over me in small circles, teasing me even more before arching her back, bringing my hands up to cup her breasts.

My thumbs trace circles around her nipples,

pinching the gorgeous, dusty pink buds between my fingers into hard, little points. I sit up on the mattress, her legs still splayed on either side of my thighs. I run my hands up her back, drawing her closer to me so I can take those very buds into my mouth. She moans, her head falling back as she continues to roll her hips over my throbbing, denim-clad dick.

"Please. Please Nico, I need you inside me. I need to feel you."

With my arms still on her back, I roll her until she is under me. Greedy hands reach for the button on my pants and eagerly tug the zipper down. My dick, still behind my briefs, struggles to break free, and I use my forearms to hold myself up while Mina shimmies my jeans and briefs down my legs until I can fully kick out of them.

Her eyes go wide as they land on my now free cock, and her hand instinctively reaches out to trace over each of the four barbells that line the underside of my shaft.

Small fist around my cock, she gently strokes me before positioning my cock near her entrance, pushing her hips to meet me. Her wetness already coats me, and I haven't even been inside her yet.

I'm ready to bury myself to the hilt, to get lost inside Mina, when I realize I don't have a condom on.

"Fuck, hold on." She looks at me as I reach over to

the rickety IKEA nightstand I've been using since college. I slide open the drawer and fumble for a small foil packet before procuring one.

Mina takes the packet from me and expertly rolls the condom onto my shaft before situating herself back on the bed, her legs apart. I position myself back at her entrance, rubbing my dick through her folds, teasing her with my barbells while trying not to slide inside her with one fucking stroke. She eagerly brings her hips to my erection, slipping the very tip inside her soaking wet cunt.

I look at her, pure lust in those green eyes of hers as she continues to try to get me further inside of her.

"Doll, are you trying to top me from the bottom?"

She giggles, and it is intoxicating. "I have no idea what you're talking about."

Her hips buck again, but I stop her from getting any further. This time when she speaks, her voice is lower. "Nico, I don't want you to be gentle with me."

Those words push me over the edge, and in one powerful thrust, I'm inside her to my balls. She gasps beneath me, and I still, giving her just a few seconds to become accustomed to my size before I begin to pump into her beautiful pussy.

Being inside her is fucking heaven. She's the kind of

woman that sonnets are written about, that songs are sung about, and right now, she's fucking mine.

All. Fucking. Mine.

I want to come so badly that I force myself to go through a mental list of anything that turns me off to keep from erupting right away.

Dirty feet.

Small dogs being carried in designer bags.

The word moist.

Mina breaks the verbal silence between us with one word that drives me to the absolute brink of insanity.

"Harder."

Fuck. Me.

My dirty little doll wants it harder.

I bend towards her face, still inside of her, and absolutely ravage her mouth with mine. Then, without warning, I slide an arm under her, flipping her to her stomach. I pull her back until she is on her knees in front of me, that luscious ass just begging to be spanked. She throws her hair over her shoulder, and I take in her back that is marred with scratches from being up against the brick wall of the bar. She looks back at me with hooded eyes, and when I meet them with mine, I slam back into her tight pussy.

Over and over again, I pound into her, my fingers digging into her hips where I'm certain she'll be bruised tomorrow. She drops her head, her breathing turning into pants, but I drop my hand from her hip to fist it hard in her hair, bringing her head back with a moan.

It's raw and primal and rough, and in this very moment I know that I'll never be able to walk away from this fucking woman.

I start to feel her walls contracting and need so badly for this woman to come that I reach around to bring a hand to her clit and slowly start to rub while I continue to thrust into her. With every thrust forward, she bucks back, wanting to be even closer and more full of my cock.

I feel my own release building at the base of my spine as Mina begins to come apart in front of me. Sweat is glistening on her back, her hair is rumpled and knotted, and her tiny hands fist into my bed sheets.

My name is like a mantra on her lips as it spills from her over and over again as her cum leaks out around my cock. I thrust forward several more times in long brutal strokes, as I find my own release deep inside her.

We're both still for several minutes, panting while trying to chase the orgasms that were torn from our bodies as they wrack with spasms. I'm still buried inside of her with my now half-hard cock. She's still on her knees in front of me, her face pressed against the mattress. I slide out of her and gently bring her to her side, pulling her body flush with mine.

We lay for several long minutes, and I reach over to wrap her in a duvet as she begins to tremble before I gently extract myself from the bed and walk to the bathroom to dispose of the condom.

I'm only gone for about a minute, but by the time I come back, Mina's breathing has evened out, and the softest snore comes from where she is curled in a ball on my bed.

I pause for only a second before I lean down and place a kiss on her forehead before walking around to the opposite side of the bed. I carefully crawl in next to her, not wanting to wake my sleeping little doll.

Our night replays in my head. Actually, every interaction I've had with her from the moment I laid eyes on her at the airport plays out like a movie, and I realize then just how fucked I truly am.

But I don't want to push her away. I don't want her just for the thrill of the chase. I only want to pull her closer to me.

So, I do just that.

I pull her closer to me and am surprised when she winds herself around me, settling back into an easy sleep. I bend to place a small kiss on the top of her head, the smell of sweat and sex and Mina swirling around the room.

I close my eyes and sigh as sleep begins to overtake me, aware of Mina's gentle breathing next to me. I know she's asleep, that she won't hear me, but before I fall asleep, I can't help but utter the words that I need her to hear. The words that one day, I'll be brave enough to say to her face instead of to her body while she sleeps so beautifully next to me.

"I think I'm falling in love with you, Mina."

Eleven

MINA

I WAKE Sunday morning in a tangle of sheets and limbs with a snoring giant pressed up against me. Somewhere between the best sex of my life and the best sleep I've had in years, I vaguely remember Nico whispering in the dark.

He's falling in love with me?

It's been less than two months since I met Nico, two months since I came home. I still have a shop in Portland, still have friends on the west coast, still have a life there. I don't know if I'm ready to make Johnson Creek my permanent home, the place I tried so hard to avoid when I was younger. I don't know if I am ready to make Nico my permanent home either.

I delicately untangle myself from him, and after a

quick look around the room, pull the white tee he wore last night over my head. I make my way down the stairs while using my emergency hair tie that is always on my wrist to pile my hair into a bun on top of my head.

I find the kitchen and thank the Gods when I spot a coffee pot tucked into one corner. Filling the reservoir with water and scooping grounds into the brewing chamber, I set out to find mugs and sugar.

I search the cabinets, finding mugs that look like they belong at The Living Room before locating a small bag of sugar in the pantry. Looking around, I can tell Nico doesn't spend much time in the kitchen. Maybe it's because he is still in the middle of renovating the place or maybe it's because he prefers takeout. I'm guessing the latter by the number of to-go menus I've found while looking for the mugs and sugar.

I sit on an old barstool, my coffee in hand before really looking around the kitchen. There is a lot of work that needs to be done - updated cabinets, paint, floors, appliances- but it really is a beautiful space. There is more than enough room for double wall ovens, room for an additional sink on the island, maybe even a wine fridge built into a lower cabinet.

For a moment, I can picture it filled with a bustling family. There is a beautiful, large window over the sink, and as I gaze outside towards the creek, I can picture kids in the backyard, a dog sniffing around, and maybe even a few chickens. I imagine what it would be like to have family dinners in this kitchen around a large, farmhouse table. I picture dancing around the kitchen while cooking those dinners, what it would be like to bake birthday cakes and cookies at Christmas. I imagine love permeating throughout the entire house, and for the briefest of seconds Nico is part of that fantasy.

He chooses that moment to come into the kitchen, a pair of basketball shorts slung tantalizingly low across his hips. I watch him cross the kitchen and pour coffee into a mug I had left out for him before he turns and walks back to me. He takes a large gulp of his coffee and makes a face akin to a toddler tasting broccoli for the first time before setting the mug down next to me and wrapping me in a hug from behind.

"Want to know a secret?" His voice is low and gravelly from sleep as he speaks into my ear.

I respond with a nod, expecting something deeply profound or extremely sexy.

"I really hate coffee," he says.

I turn to face him, a look of bewilderment on my face. In return, he gives me a small shrug before the corners of his lips quirk up into a smile, and suddenly, we both start laughing.

"But," I start while still laughing, "you have a coffee pot. And you drank coffee with me at the diner?"

The biggest grin creeps up over his face. "I was keeping up appearances. I wanted you to like me."

His vulnerability takes me aback, and I feel a small vise tighten around my heart.

His arms come around me and wrap me in a hug, the growing scruff on his face scratching my neck.

We order breakfast from the local diner and feast on pancakes, French toast, and fresh fruit from the comfort of Nico's bed.

I'm telling Nico about my plans to help my nieces redo their bathroom, and he laughs while we commiserate over the creepy Minnie Mouse shower curtain in the kids' bathroom. He has spent many nights over the last several years crashing in the guest room, the room that is now mine, so he knows the bathroom well.

"I have an idea," he says, and I laugh because almost every bad idea I've ever had started with someone uttering that exact phrase. "Let's take the girls to IKEA."

I protest, knowing that I surely cannot be seen out in public in the outfit I was wearing last night, but after some coaxing from Nico, I agree to the trip. Instead of backtracking to my brother's house to change and grab the girls, Nico calls Colin to see if he would bring the girls and clothes for me while I jump in the shower.

I'm only in the shower for a few minutes when I hear the door to the bathroom open. I peer out the quickly fogging glass door to find a fully naked Nico with two towels in hand. "They'll be here in about an hour. Mind if I join you in there?"

I crack open the door, a silent answer to his question, and then, he is there with me. The small shower immediately feels even more cramped than it was when I climbed in, but it isn't because there is an additional person in the space. Instead, it is the heat that radiates between us that permeates the shower stall, almost making it hard for me to catch my breath.

While I have had relationships and hookups in my past, I don't think that any of my previous lovers have been as attentive as Nico is.

He adjusts the water and looks to me for confirmation that it isn't too hot. Then, without hesitation, he positions me so the water sprays over my hair and body. He reaches out, taking a bottle of shampoo before gently lathering my scalp and hair, massaging his fingers into my skin. I laugh nervously and profusely apologize when I notice that his hands and all the lather around me are tinted pink- a hazard of unnatural hair colors. I'm afraid they will stain, and when I tell him so, he lets out a boisterous laugh.

"Look at this shower. Do you really think I plan on

keeping these baby blue tiles that haven't been in style since sometime in the late 80s?"

He continues to wash me under the spray of the shower, talking about his plans for the house while he rubs conditioner from my roots to the tip of my strands. Our trip to IKEA today will be for his benefit as much as mine and my nieces.

After rinsing the conditioner from my hair, he grabs a loofa from a hook on the wall and adds a generous amount of shower gel to it, working it into a rich lather. The smell of pine and fresh mountain air hangs thick in the air. It is the scent of Nico.

"Sorry; it's all I have," he says sheepishly when he sees me inhaling the scent deeply.

"No, it's okay. It smells like you." I pause for a second before continuing, "I like it."

He smiles at me, one of those beautifully wicked smiles that would make any straight woman drop her panties on the spot, and I let myself bask in the fact that right now, I'm the woman he is smiling at.

As we stand in the shower, he brings the loofa to my neck, running it over my body. He trails down my chest, circling each breast with the sponge, my nipples pebbling with each swipe. With one hand on my shoulder, he works his way lower and lower, over my stomach, turning me away from him to work over my back and ass. He kneels before me, lifting one foot to sit on his thigh while he washes from my toes to the top of my thigh before repeating the process with my other leg. Both my feet come back to the tile floor, and while still on his knees, he edges my feet wider. Coating his hands with the lather of the loofa, he slides them between my legs, gently running them over my now throbbing pussy before taking me by surprise, reaching behind my legs, sliding one hand between my ass cheeks.

I gasp, and as his face turns up towards me, our eyes meeting under the spray of water, he groans out his words, "One day, I'm going to take your pretty little ass for myself."

He grazes one finger over the tight, puckered skin before sliding his hand back through my legs, his palm grazing my pussy as he does. "Even under all this water I can feel how wet you are for me, Mina."

I shudder as he rinses me and places one kiss above my pussy before slowly kissing his way up my stomach until he is standing in front of me. His cock is hard against me as he kisses my mouth, his hand in that now comforting, possessive hold on the back of my neck.

In this moment, I want to touch him more than I have ever wanted anything before. No, I don't want to touch him- I *need* to touch him.

Giving caution to the slippery tile, I gently press

myself against him and walk him backwards until his back is against the tiled wall. Hands on his chest, I drop to my knees in front of him, sending a silent prayer to the Gods that I don't slip and fall.

Lust is swirling in his eyes like a hurricane when he looks down at me. "You don't have..." he starts, but I cut him off.

"I want to."

His gaze stays locked with mine, and his nostrils flare as I trace my fingers up and down his shaft before taking him in my fist. I give his cock a few long pumps, licking my lips before taking him into my mouth. I want to be delicate and soft, but right now, I need him too much. I need to show him how I feel by giving him this.

I lick his cock, playing with the barbells that pierce the underside of his shaft. I lick from his root to his tip, swirling my tongue around him before lightly grazing his head with my teeth.

"Fuck, Mina," his hands come down to the back of my head, "that feels incredible."

His words spur me on, and I continue to feast on him, taking as much of him into my mouth as I can. I glance up at him. His head is thrown back, muscles cording in his neck, and I am overcome with pure desire. I relax my jaw, and he slips further into my mouth, hitting the back of my throat.

The water runs cold over our bodies, and I notice that I'm shivering, but I can't stop. I need to taste him. My eyes water as he tightens the grip on my hair, holding my head from behind as he begins to unabashedly thrust into my mouth. I steady myself with one hand while bringing my other to palm his balls, lightly tugging as he groans above me.

His release is near, and he tries to push me back, tries to escape my mouth, but all I want is to taste him. I reach my arms between him and the tiled wall and grab his ass with my hands, nails digging into his skin, holding him inside me. Our eyes meet for a millisecond, and I give him as much of a nod as I can muster with his cock between my lips.

He fucks my mouth with reckless abandon, real tears now coming from my eyes as slurping sounds from my spit and shower water mix around us and reverberate off the shower walls. He pulls even harder on my hair, making my scalp tingle, and when I whimper around his cock, he comes in my mouth in hard spurts, a salty mix of cum and sweat and a distinct taste that is simply Nico.

He stills, slowly releasing the grip on my hair, the blood flow returning to my scalp, before reaching over and shutting off the water. Nico then pulls me to my feet and leads me from the shower where he wraps me in one of the huge, oversized towels he brought into the bathroom with him. He rubs my arms, partly to warm me up, partly in reassurance before dropping his forehead to mine.

"You make me want to lose control," he growls.

I laugh, pressing my lips to his before turning and walking back to his bedroom. Only when I'm alone in his room do I sit at the edge of the bed and think to myself that he has already made me lose my own control.

Twelve

Nico

THERE IS a special place in hell for the type of people who go furniture shopping on a Sunday at IKEA just a few weeks before college starts back up for the year. And today, I'm one of those people.

I can't exactly be mad; I mean, it was my idea. But now, as we wander the endless maze of the showroom floor, somewhere between the Poang chairs and Hemnes dressers, I am confident that I have absolutely lost any small semblance of sanity I had.

My motives for our little group outing may have been partly selfish. I wasn't ready for my weekend with Mina to be over yet. I also was quickly learning that I couldn't survive out of boxes in the long term and desperately wanted to move as quickly as possible to finish my house- without sacrificing quality, of course.

The floors would be complete this week and I was ready to move into the larger project of the kitchen. I was also ready to have the entire project contracted out so I could stay locked away in my bedroom between the legs of the woman who was walking next to me.

Emily and Laurel ran ahead to the next showcase room, a giant "See What You Can Do With Just 680 Square Feet" plastered on the side of the display room. They were having a blast exploring the rooms, looking for inspiration for exactly what they wanted to do to their new "grown-up" bathroom, often asking Mina for her suggestions. I think one of them mentioned the phrase "Pinterest worthy," and while I had no idea what the fuck that meant, I can only assume that it is something very important to teenage girls.

The entire time, I can't help but watch how Mina interacts with the girls. She was incredibly great with them, and of course, I can't help but think how she would be with her own child one day. Our child. I could imagine her body transforming during pregnancy, her breasts growing larger and more tender, her stomach swelling as she protected the tiny being forming inside her...

"Nico?" Her voice jolted me back to the present as she waved a hand in front of my face to get my attention.

"I'm sorry; I must have zoned out there," I replied with a shaky laugh. "What's up?"

She looked at me questioningly before pointing towards a gray and white kitchen. We walk over to the kitchen model, and I watch as Mina starts to explore the drawers and cabinets. It was huge and open, a giant island in the middle of the space with a small sink perfect for washing vegetables and an easy to access dishwasher directly under the sink. An oven and microwave were built into one side while the opposite held a gas stove. Along the back wall, a large farmhouse sink was flanked with frosted glass uppers. She ran her hands over the smooth, granite countertop and when I caught her eyes, she smiled, but for perhaps the first time, her smile didn't reach her eyes.

"We should catch up with the girls." She hurriedly walks away, leaving me alone with a bowl of fake lemons and a barrage of small kitchen spice jars that were scattered around the space.

I don't hurry to meet back up with Mina, Emily, and Laurel, believing that perhaps she needs some space, even if that is the last thing I want to give her. I knew I wanted Mina from the very second that I laid eyes on her at the airport, and it scared the shit out of me how quickly I had fallen head over fucking heels for this woman. Suddenly, I don't want to just flip my house to make a buck off of it. I want to finish the renovation. I want to move Mina in with me. I want to dance to Mumford & Sons in the kitchen with her on a Sunday morning. I want to marry her and have babies with her and spend every minute of the rest of my life worshiping her.

I exhale, shaking the idea from my mind as I catch back up with the girls just before they disappear to the marketplace, bypassing the Swedish meatballs calling my name from the restaurant so oddly tucked in the middle of the store. Emily runs to grab a shopping cart that has the worst steering in the history of all shopping carts while Laurel looks at a selection of cheap "buy-me-now" merchandise, holding up a Bolmen, a toilet brush to the layperson, to Mina before tossing it in the cart.

I grab Mina's hand. "Hey."

"Hey," she replies, the same not-fully-there smile crossing her lips but not reaching her eyes.

"Are we good?"

She nods, but I'm not sure I believe her.

We wind through the rest of the marketplace, ending up with a new shower curtain (cursed Minnie Mouse be gone!) towels, bathmats, some organizing thingy with a million vowels in its name that I don't even try to pronounce, a few fake plants and candles, as well as artwork and frames. I grab some outdoor furniture for my place, as well as a deep navy, velvet couch and two dark-green, wing-back chairs while already silently cursing the thought of trying to assemble the things.

One of the girls throws a pack of cinnamon rolls on the belt as we're checking out, and I give her a silent fist bump of approval.

After we check out, I bring my truck to the loading zone, Mina stuffing oversized blue IKEA bags into the back seat of the truck between the girls while I throw box after box of furniture into the bed of the truck.

We arrive back at Colin's house, and as Mina is getting ready to jump to the ground, Emily speaks up from the back.

"Uncle Nico,' she squeaks, sounding younger than she is. "Can you come in and have a cinnamon roll with us?"

I've never been so thankful for that girl as I am at that moment since I'm fairly certain Mina was getting ready to give me the cold shoulder. But still, I look to Mina before seeking her approval first, which she gives me with a small nod.

I help the girls collect their purchases from the truck and follow them into Colin's house as the girls run to find him and Pauli, eager to show them their new bathroom decor.

We all meet up in the kitchen, huge carb-loaded, sugar-laden rolls being passed around. Mina's purse from the night before sits on the kitchen counter, and it catches her eye when a text alert chirps.

"Philly," Colin says, and I don't miss the small eye roll she gives at the nickname, "I have no idea what is going on, but that thing has been blaring all day. Seriously, why don't you keep it on silent like everyone else?"

Mina turns her attention to her purse, digging until she pulls her phone from its depths. As she scrolls through her phone, every ounce of color drains from her face, and she starts to shake as tears stream down her face.

"Mina," I say.

"Mina," Colin repeats deeper when she doesn't respond to me. Slowly, she hands the phone to her brother as she sinks to the floor, and I can see the rage bubbling up to Colin's surface.

Matt: *I'm not done with you yet.*

Matt: *I know where you are, you little slut.*

Matt: *You think you can leave me, but you can't.*

Matt: *I'm coming for you.*

Along with at least twenty other texts in varying

degrees of escalation, Mina's phone shows she has missed 32 phone calls from Matt along with several voicemail messages and texts from Daphne begging Mina to call her as soon as possible.

Colin is talking to Pauli in the corner, I assume filling her in on what has happened while the girls look on wide-eyed and slightly terrified as their aunt crumbles to the ground before them. I've been in their shoes, losing a parent young, and I feel for them knowing that in this moment, their young minds must be going bonkers thinking of every worst case scenario possible. I'm torn between running to Mina and making sure the girls are okay. I rapidly motion them over to me, putting a hand on each of their shoulders as I bend down to look at them. "I know what you're probably thinking right now, that something terrible has happened or that something terrible is going to happen to someone you love." Even if I don't fully believe the words coming out of my mouth, I continue, "Everything is okay; everything is going to be okay."

Because it has to be okay. I won't let anything happen to her - to the woman I love. Because yes, I fucking love her.

The girls, seeming pacified, quickly move to the living room with Pauli. I move to Mina, quietly lowering myself to sit next to her on the cold floor. I place my hand on her back, but her entire body tenses, face whipping around to turn to me as if my touch burned her skin. My hands come up in front of me. The last thing she needs right now is to feel threatened.

Colin sinks down on the opposite side of her, meeting my eyes, but not dismissing me as I expected him to do. We sit in silence for long minutes, the only sound coming from Mina's occasional sobs as she hugs her legs in front of her.

When she finally looks up, she looks like a completely different person. Her eyes, red-rimmed from crying, don't have her normal sparkle, and instead of the usual joy that reflects in them, all I see is hurt and deep pain. Her skin is flushed, red blotches spreading across her chest. Her bottom lip has teeth marks in it from how hard she has been biting it.

She looks so small and so broken, and yet, she is still just as stunning as she was the first time I met her. And while I don't know the entire story, all I want to do is wrap her in my arms and carry her somewhere safe while promising her that this fucking monster of a man will never threaten her again. But I know she doesn't need me to do that right now, that she may even be afraid of me right now, afraid of all men right now.

I stand and walk to Colin, placing a hand on his shoulder, a silent understanding passing between us that he could call me night or day and I would be there for him - for Mina.

But before I can walk out of the kitchen, a small broken voice breaks through the silence in shuddering sobs. "Nico, Please stay."

Thirteen

MINA

My mind is a mess. My emotions are bouncing around in my body like a pinball being rocketed towards a high score. The only thing I am sure of is that I want Nico here beside me.

No; I'm suddenly aware that I *need* him here beside me.

He slowly sits back on the ground. I place a tentative hand on his thigh while taking my brother's hand on the other side of me. Right now, I need both of these strong men as my bookends, keeping me from toppling.

I sit in silence for several more minutes with them, willing myself to speak without my voice cracking. And then, I tell them everything.

I tell them about my relationship with Matt.

How he started out *so* sweet.

How he became mean.

How he would monitor my text messages and social media accounts.

How he once hit me.

How I had a black eye that I had to cover with makeup and oversized sunglasses.

How Colin had texted me the next day, and I left Portland, not only wanting to be here for him and the girls, but to escape Matt as well.

I tell them everything. And my voice does crack as I speak. More tears fall, and I feel utterly exhausted, broken, and depleted.

When I finish, my brother stands to move to the refrigerator, pulling three beers from the door. He returns to the floor, passing one across me to Nico before handing one to me as well.

Nico breaks the silence first. "I want to *kill* the mother fucker." His words come out clipped, fueled by anger.

Colin, ever the attorney, nods before adding, "play the crime of passion angle and a jury might let you off easy."

I look to my left, then my right, and suddenly, sandwiched between my brother and his best friend, I feel so protected, so cherished, that I can't help but laugh despite the pain I feel. I laugh long and hard until tears are spilling from my eyes, and they are both looking at me like I've gone absolutely crazy.

Maybe I have.

"No one is killing anyone. I won't have either of you ending up in prison on my account."

I reach for my phone to text Daphne.

Mina: *I'm sorry I didn't have my phone with me. Are you free to talk?*

In true Daphne fashion, my screen immediately illuminates with a FaceTime request, and I swipe to answer, her words spilling out the second the video call connects. "Ohmygod Mina, I was so worried about you…"

But then, she goes quiet, and her eyes widen as she looks first at my tear stained face and then to the men on either side of me.

"My brother, Colin," I point my head towards him, "and his best friend, Nico," I say as I swing my head in the other direction.

"Well hell, Mina. I knew that one was hot," she points to Nico, "but you never told me your brother was so sexy!"

Colin sits in a silent fit of laughter next to me, Nico waving and throwing in a "Nice to meet you," before taking a long pull from his beer all the while I sit in stunned silence, willing us to get back to the point of our call.

Eventually, I get Daphne back on track, and she tells me that Matt showed up at our Portland tattoo shop late Saturday evening yelling at her while reeking of alcohol. He demanded to know where I was and when she wouldn't tell him, he threatened to burn our shop down before storming out of the shop as quickly as he had come in.

I filled her in on the text messages and missed phone calls from him. "Oh, honey, I'm sorry you are still dealing with this mess of a man. I swear if he comes anywhere near you or our shop, I'll chop his balls off."

Her tone is serious, and both Nico and Colin grimace.

We say our goodbyes, Daphne telling my brother that he should call her sometime, and as soon as the screen goes black, the three of us burst into fits of giggles.

"That woman," Colin starts before just shaking his head.

I stand, wanting to call Thom to give him a heads up of what is happening in case we need to do anything different at the shop here, but Colin tells me to stay, that he will make the phone call for me. In that moment, I am thankful for my big brother, thankful for one less thing I have to worry about in this giant mess of my life.

And suddenly, it is just Nico and me in the kitchen. He pushes off the floor, coming to stand inches from me.

"Can I hug you?" His voice is a low whisper.

I smile because the man is so incredibly sweet. He is caring and knows boundaries and respect, but he still seems to love with his entire heart. And then, there is the sex. Yes, I know I'm fragile and vulnerable right now and that is the last thing I should be thinking about, but when you are with someone that makes you feel so safe and secure, everything else just seems to fall into place, amazing sex included.

"Please," I whisper, nodding.

And he hugs me. Oh, does he hug me. He wraps his arms around me, pulling me to his chest, and we stay that way, slowly breathing together in an embrace that says so much more than words ever could in the moment.

We only pull away when Colin returns, me sheepishly backing away from Nico as if we have been caught doing something we shouldn't be doing.

"Philly."

I look at Colin, unsure.

"I'm okay." He glances between us. "I love you," he points towards me, "and I always will. And that fool," he gestures to Nico, "well, I kind of love him, too. You suit each other well."

I hug my brother as he speaks directly to Nico. "Dude, you break her heart, and I'll break your fucking pretty boy face."

A whoop of laughter escapes my lips, never having heard my prim and proper brother talk like that before.

Colin excuses himself to go talk to my mom. Upon his departure, I am suddenly aware that my body feels like it has just finished a marathon. I am utterly exhausted.

It's nowhere near time to go to sleep, but I simply don't care. My body craves soft clothes, bedsheets, and gentle music. And it craves the strong body of the man I am falling for.

"Would you lay with me for a little while - just until I fall asleep?"

The soft smile he aims at me is magnetic as he reaches up to my face, his palm caressing my cheek, "Doll, I'll lay with you for as long as you want."

I ascend the stairs, the energy I need to keep propelling myself forward draining with every step. I reach the last step, and my legs give out from beneath me, but strong arms come around my waist before I hit the floor, and I am suddenly swept into Nico's strong arms.

He cradles me in those arms as he carries me to my room. Cradled against his strong chest, I hold onto him like he is a life raft, and I'm adrift at sea.

When we enter my room, he sets me gently onto the mattress, and I direct him to my small closet for a change of clothes. When he returns with them in hand, he simply looks at me and asks, "Do you trust me?"

I nod, because I do trust him. I trust him fully.

He strips me bare, but he doesn't try to do anything other than to place a chaste kiss on my lips. He dresses me in pajama pants and a matching tank top before pulling me to my feet long enough to lower the covers on the bed before placing me softly back on my bed.

He turns on a gentle Spotify station and the sounds of "One and Only" by Adele sweeps around the room. The song seems to speak every word that's on my mind.

Nico removes his shoes and crawls into the tiny bed next to me, holding me flush against his body, my face nuzzled under his chin. So tenderly, he runs his fingers through my hair, and when tears spill from my eyes once again, he uses the pad of his thumb to wipe them away.

Leaning down, he places a kiss to the top of my head before chanting a chorus of affirmations against my hair with each additional kiss.

"You're safe with me."

Kiss.

"I won't let anything happen to you, Mina."

Kiss.

"You are so strong."

Kiss.

"You are so incredibly brave and beautiful, Mina."

Kiss.

And somewhere in these mantras spilling from his tender lips, I start to believe every word he says to me.

I'm seconds away from being overtaken with sleep, exhausted from the rollercoaster of emotions battling within my brain, but I can't let another minute pass without telling this man how I feel about him, that I feel for him what he feels for me.

"Nico," I rasp, my voice heavy with sleep.

I feel him kiss the top of my head once more in response, a small murmur coming from his lips. And before I fall into my dreams, I link my fingers together with his and give him my heart.

"I think I'm falling in love with you, too."

Fourteen

Nico

Shortly after eleven that night, I wake, still clinging to Mina as she sleeps. This bed is painfully small, almost childlike. I've crashed in this bed many times in the past after nights of drinking way too much with Colin and our friends in the backyard. Maybe I've always been too drunk to notice how tiny it was before. Still, I know that isn't the reason I hold onto Mina like she is my only saving grace from falling off the edge. She is God personified, and I simply stare at her sleeping frame, thinking back to the words she said to me before drifting sweetly off to sleep.

She's falling in love with me, too. Sure, she had an extremely stressful day thanks to that asshole of an ex, but maybe she wasn't just overcome with emotion in the moment. Maybe she did mean it when she said it. Maybe she is starting to feel the same way I do, starting to feel the undeniable pull we have to each other.

I extract myself from the bed, pulling the covers closer around her before I quietly leave the room and walk downstairs in need of a drink. I knew I had Colin's permission to pursue Mina at The Living Room, but I was still flooded with relief when he again gave his blessing to both of us tonight. In all honesty, I had pictured my first sleepover with Mina in this house before, and it sure as hell didn't end with me traipsing through the kitchen, making myself a sandwich and pouring a glass of some crappy soymilk alternative. I always assumed I would be jumping out of her bedroom window or running out the front door fully naked with Colin throwing anything he could get his hands on at me, screaming at me to stay away from his sister.

A light is on in the living room, and I walk towards it expecting to find Colin, only to be surprised to find Pauli sitting in an armchair, the dog snoring softly at her feet. She's doing something that upon closer inspection turns out to be a crossword puzzle. When she sees me in the doorway, she motions for me to join her, and I do, taking my plate and sitting in the chair next to her.

There aren't a lot of things in life that scare me. I'm six foot four and covered in tattoos. I work out regularly to maintain my toned body, and for the most part, I watch what I eat. But Pauline "Pauli" Pappas scares the ever living fuck out of me. If there were a large, organized crime population in Johnson Creek, I am fairly certain she would be the head of it. Hell, maybe her little woman's auxiliary club is just a front.

She has never blatantly said that she doesn't like me, but the woman has thrown more than enough daggers my way over the years that words haven't been needed.

Her eyes narrow over the frames of her designer reader glasses as she stares at me, long seconds ticking past on the grandfather clock in the corner of the room. I don't speak, and neither does she. After several more tense moments of silence, she returns to her crossword puzzle while speaking.

"Do you love her?"

"Yes," I respond immediately, my voice nothing but a mere whisper.

Silence stretches between us once again. I haven't touched my sandwich; my drink remains untouched as well.

She stands to leave, Stella following closely at her heels, and just when I think she is going to walk out of the room, Pauli turns to look at me again, her gaze slightly softer this time. "I don't like to admit when I am wrong, Nicolas, but I think I might have been wrong about you."

Pauli walks out of the room, leaving me alone with only my thoughts, the sound of the grandfather clock ticking in the distance, and the biggest fucking grin on my face.

———

It's been a few weeks since that night on the kitchen floor of Colin's house, and in the time that has passed, Mina and I have become increasingly closer. Neither of us have expressed our love to one another in words, but we do it almost daily with our actions- our stolen glances, our playful touching, and the intimate moments we share. And there are a lot of intimate moments.

It's mid-August and the humidity still hangs thick in the air as Mina pulls into the driveway in the rusted, old Mustang she purchased earlier this week. I never would have thought my girl would be into old muscle cars, but she still finds ways to surprise me every day.

The inside of the house has almost been finished, and today, with Mina's help, we are going to tackle some much needed landscaping. I've been pulling weeds and fertilizing the lawn throughout the summer, and my work is starting to pay off with lush grass stretching from the front yard to the creek lining the rear of the property.

Mina climbs from the car, and it's suddenly hard to breathe. She wears the same black shorts she was wearing the day that I surprised her when she was covered in pink hair color and a barely there sports bra that stretches tightly over her tits. Her hair is up in a messy bun, and she doesn't have a stitch of makeup on her beautiful, round face.

She bounds towards me where I stand in the bed of my truck surrounded by plants and small trees, and when she nears, I reach down, pulling her into the bed of my truck and into my arms. It's so fucking cute when she pushes up on her toes to kiss my lips with hers. She's long legs and slender hips, and she's mine.

We work through much of the morning and into the late afternoon, music coming from the portable speaker on the edge of the porch. We plant daffodils, cosmos, and phlox, bringing color to the once stagnant green blanketing the lawn. Mina eventually disappears into the house, emerging several minutes later with two glasses of lemonade.

After long, cool drinks, we finish up, me grabbing the last few flowers from the bed of my truck as Mina digs small holes in the earth, instructing me where to place each one. I love working in tandem with her, always falling into step with one another, each of us learning to anticipate each other's moves.

As the last of the flowers are placed in the ground, we work together to replace the dirt around the base of each clump until a sudden rumble reverberates across the sky and rain begins to pour from above. It soaks us in seconds, cascading down around our bodies. I look at Mina, expecting her to run for cover on the porch, but instead, she reaches her arms out wide and tilts her head up to the skies, letting the water run over the length of her body as she spins in carefree circles.

"Unsteady" begins playing over the speaker, and when she stops spinning, she looks to me, her eyes full of lust. "Nico," she almost yells to be heard over the combination of rain and music, "dance with me!"

I take long strides across the lawn to meet her, and then, we dance. I pull her into my arms, our bodies pressed against one another. We sway together, surrounded by the downpour and sounds of thunder rumbling around us. I slant my mouth over hers, capturing her lips with mine. A moan escapes her lips, and I immediately feel myself growing hard. She feels it, too, and she deepens our kiss.

This moment feels so fucking perfect and real that I can't hold back any longer. I break our kiss, sliding my hands up her body to cup her face. She nuzzles a cheek into my palm, and I look into her eyes, a huge smile pulling my lips.

And then, I tell her.

"I love you, Mina. I fucking love you so much."

Best of all, she doesn't even hesitate before saying it back. And when she does, it takes my breath away. "Oh, Nico," she says breathlessly, "I love you too!"

We stay there in the rain for several more minutes, simply holding each other until our hands begin to rove each other's bodies. Mina's tiny hands slide up my chest as mine slide down her back, gripping her ass. I lift her up, her legs instinctively wrapping around my waist. I drop my forehead to hers and pressed together, fused as one, I carry her inside the house that is quickly becoming home.

I don't even make it to the bedroom. I set her down on the stairs just inside the front door. She arches her hips as I drag her sopping wet shorts down her legs, surprised to find she isn't wearing any panties. Her arms go over her head, and I strip her sports bra from her body, stepping back to take in the full view of her beautiful curves.

Her breasts heave as her breathing becomes labored, lust flashing in her eyes. Mina surprises me every day, and today is no exception. Without warning, she speaks, commanding me to take off my clothes in a voice more authoritative than her usual, chipper tone. She holds my eyes and as I reach to pull off my shirt, still clinging to my body from the rain, she trails her hands down over her breasts, pushing them together before letting them fall heavily apart.

Shirt now added to the growing pile of dank clothing littering the floor, I go to reach for her, but she shakes her head, pointing to my bottoms.

"All of it," she rasps.

As I drag my shorts down my body, her hands begin to slide down her own again, this time only skimming her tits before she continues to gravitate towards her pussy. She toys with the short, blonde curls that cover her mound before splaying the lips of her cunt with her fingers, giving me an unobstructed view of how fucking wet she is for me.

A growl escapes from my throat. "God damnit. What are you doing to me, Mina?"

Without answering, she slides her fingers through her slick folds, coating them with her wetness. I close in on her, needing to be closer. I'm transfixed under the spell this woman has cast on me, and when she holds her fingers up to me, slicked with her juices, I waste no time taking them between my lips to savor her taste.

I bend to her, taking her mouth with mine. I reach

for her body, but she reaches out to circle a delicate hand around my wrist while pushing me away with her other hand.

"Watch me," she pants. "I want you to watch me."

I stand back, fire in my veins, and I watch as she slides her fingers back to her cunt. She glides her fingers through her folds before settling on her clit, drawing small circles around the nub. Her other hand circles her breast, teasing her nipple into a tight, little bud.

Her gaze drops from my eyes to my cock, painfully throbbing and standing more than fully erect. My hand drops to it, wrapping a fist around its thickness as Mina looks on, giving me a small nod of approval.

One of her fingers dips into her pussy, a small moan escaping her lips at its entrance, and I'm immediately jealous of that fucking finger. She thrusts her hips off the stairs, circling them as she slides an additional finger inside her pussy. I close the space between us, standing to straddle her, stroking my dick on top of her.

My pace quickens, but before I can lose total control, Mina's other hand reaches out and takes my hand from my cock leaving it to bob up and down on its own several times before standing rigid at attention. My hand in hers, she guides it to her soaking cunt, but doesn't allow me to replace her own fingers. Instead, she grinds onto my palm several times, leaving her wetness all over my hand, before pushing it away from her and placing my hand back on my cock.

Holy. Fucking. Shit.

This woman. My woman. My woman who loves me and puts fucking porn stars to shame just coated me in her wetness and is instructing me to jerk off, coated with her juices.

I've never been so turned on in my life.

I furiously fist myself, my eyes continuing to drift over Mina's body. I don't know that there is anything sexier than watching her body squirm under her own ministrations. Sweat beads on her brow, and her breathing hitches as moans pour from her lips. It only urges me on, an orgasm building in the base of my spine.

Her face looks beautifully pained as she edges closer to her own release, her other hand coming out to grab my hip, nails digging into my skin. She speaks, a small whimper barely escaping her trembling lips, "Nico, come with me."

That's all I need to hear from her, and mere seconds later I find my release, coating her chest and stomach in thick, hot ropes of cum as she bucks her hips under me, coming undone. I grunt as the last bit leaves my cock, and then watch in surprise as Mina runs a finger through the sticky aftermath of my orgasm. She brings the finger to her lips, sucking it clean before rubbing more of my come over her body.

A satisfied smile crosses her lips, and I notice she is staring at my dick, already half hard, already wanting more.

Still naked, I pull her up from the stairs, kissing her deep, entwining our souls with lust and love. I carry her up the stairs and into the now fully renovated primary suite, crossing into the large bathroom she helped me pick out materials for.

A large, white freestanding tub stands in the middle of an oversized Carrara tiled shower. Multiple shower heads jut out from the wall and ceiling. A tile bench is built into the back wall, and a built-in tile shelf holds an assortment of shampoos, conditioners, and body washes.

Without putting her down, I adjust the water to the tub, adding some of the fancy bubble bath she insists on keeping here. Then, as the water rises, I cautiously step into the tub, Mina still in my arms, and lower us both into the water.

We sit in silence, her between my legs as I use a loofah to gently scrub her back. When it falls into the sudsy water around us, Mina leans back into me, a blissful sigh escaping her lips as I turn her head towards me and kiss her gently. We lay together like this, my arms eventually coming to wrap around her body for almost an hour. Our fingers and toes turn into wrinkly little prunes as we simply enjoy each other's presence.

It's intimate and beautiful, and I never want it to end. But when the water begins to cool, I edge her from between my legs, and once we're both out of the tub, I wrap her in an oversized towel pulled from the towel warmer. The towel warmer is another one of Mina's touches she insisted on. When I think about it, everywhere I look in this house, small pieces of Mina's feminine style can be found. And I surprisingly don't mind it.

I wrap a towel around my waist before draining the tub, rinsing it clean of the residue of the bubble bath. I walk to the attached bedroom to find Mina stretched on top of the duvet, still wrapped in her towel. She has turned on a small essential oil diffuser, and the scent of lavender envelopes the room.

The mattress dips under my weight as I press my body to her back, bringing my arms around the woman I love, cradling her, protecting her.

She turns to face me, kissing me softly before her hand slides down my chest, unwrapping the towel from my lower half and pushing it away from my body. Her arms push her body from the bed and she climbs onto me, still wrapped in her towel, straddling me with her legs as her pussy rests dangerously close to my now hard cock.

I reach to my new and improved nightstand for a condom, but her hand comes to mine, stilling it before I can reach the drawer as she gives the slowest shake of her head.

Fifteen

MINA

With Nico's hand in mine, I look at him and see something in his eyes that tugs at my heart. Fear? Maybe uncertainty? He is always so solid, so sure of himself that seeing his features twist in conflict almost physically pains me.

"Hey," I say gently, bringing his palm up to cup my cheek in reassurance. "I don't want anything between us."

He looks at me, slightly dazed as if the words haven't fully sunk in.

I continue, "I'm on the pill. And I've always been safe. I need this, need you and only you. Nothing between us."

His eyes go wide, pupils dilating until they are

almost pure black. He reaches up to open the towel still tied around my body, and it flutters around us as his hands come to rest on my hips.

I bring a hand between us, feeling his hard length, teasing his cock with my nails before wiping away a pearl-like bead of moisture that leaked from its tip. His groans send shivers over my body and make me wet. So wet.

With a knee still on either side of his body, I position his cock near my entrance, teasing him and covering him in my wetness at the same time. I circle my hips in small figure eights, rubbing his gorgeous tip over my clit until it throbs with need. Achingly slow, I line him up with my cunt and inch myself onto his cock. Inch by inch, I take him inside my heat. Just him. Just Nico.

As I move slowly, up and down his shaft, I can feel the barbells of his piercings rub against my sensitive flesh, and I shudder at the sensation. He reaches for my hips, but I take his hands and push them above his head, leaning down and holding them there as I capture his lips with mine. Nico doesn't try to move them, sensing that I need this. I need to take control right now.

And I do. I take control as I take kisses from him, as I quicken my pace on top of him, as I nuzzle my face into the sensitive skin where his neck meets his shoulder, and bite. I watch as the skin turns red, and a groan escapes from his lips. I'm wild and uninhibited as I slide my fingers down his arms, still where I placed them on the mattress, and splay my fingers over his neck, squeezing him as I ride him. Gently at first, and with more force as he spurs me on, as he tells me it's okay with his penetrative gaze.

His hips begin to buck under me, thrusting to meet me each time I relentlessly slide up and down on his cock. My hands still around his throat, I feel each breath, each swallow as his Adam's apple tries to bob beneath my hands. He moves his arms from above the bed, and I don't push them back as he brings them to punishingly grip my hips. His short nails dig into my skin, finding purchase as he holds onto me like his life depends on it.

We move in unison as sweat clings to both of our bodies, and with several long and demanding thrusts, we come apart. We grunt and moan and thrust together. Our lips crash together violently, with teeth nipping and biting. I feel Nico pulse deep inside of me, spilling into me with no barrier between us, and it is the most wonderful feeling I've ever experienced.

My hands go limp around his neck, and I crumble into a heap on top of him, shuddering in the aftermath of a blissful orgasm. So gently, so caringly, he brings his arms around me, running his hands up and down the column of my spine, across the chakra symbols that line my back.

Nico rolls me to the side, his hands still clasped around my body. We lay chest to chest, our breathing slowly returning to normal while he peppers kisses across my lips, across my cheeks, across my eyelids.

We don't speak for what feels like hours, listening as the rain continues to pelt down on the roof above, gentle thunder rumbling in the distance. We stay clinging to one another with nothing but our hands filling the void of words.

When I finally break the silence, eyes locked to Nico's, it's only to utter two words to him. "Thank you," I say, my words barely more than a whisper.

"For what, doll?"

I'm not sure what I want to say to him, I just know that he *needs* to know how much I appreciate him. Words come out before I can stop them. "For everything, Nico. For making me feel beautiful. For actually listening when I talk. For letting me explore sides of myself that I never felt comfortable enough to explore before." My hand comes up, my knuckles brushing across his cheek. "For loving me."

"God, Mina," he pulls me closer, kissing my head and inhaling my scent. "Part of me thinks that I fell in love with you the very second I saw you in the airport terminal." I smile against him as he continues, "and if I didn't fall in love with you then, I certainly fell in love with you when you pulled that vibrator out of your bag on a plane full of people."

I laugh and playfully push him away, but he captures my wrists and pulls me back to him, tickling my sides until tears roll from my eyes, and I can't catch my breath from laughter.

I compose myself, snuggling back up to Nico, my ass now pressed against his nude body. His body is all hard and chiseled, muscle and man, yet when he holds me, I feel like I'm wrapped in the most luxurious silk ever created.

"Can I ask you something?" I crane my head to look at him over my shoulder.

He nods. "You can ask me anything, doll."

"Do you think you'll ever get married again?"

"I do," he says without hesitation, pulling me closer to him. "I fucked up a lot my first time around. I made mistakes - big mistakes. But I also learned from them and grew as a person. I'm 43 now; I know how to handle my emotions, how to give love and accept it in return. I'd love to build a family one day, even if I would be ancient by the time the kid graduates highschool."

We lounge in bed the rest of the afternoon into the early evening, simply holding each other. We share secrets, our deepest desires for the future. We share casual takeout from the comfort of the king-sized bed surrounded by pillows and reruns of old HGTV shows. And somewhere, in the middle of it all, I decide that this place, right here next to Nico, is my forever home.

———

NICO STANDS AT ONE OF THE TWO SINKS IN THE primary bathroom brushing his teeth while dressed in relaxed fitting dress pants and a button up dress shirt as I bound into the room, practically giddy with excitement. "Party in the USA" blares over the speaker in his bedroom, and he laughs, his mouth full of toothpaste, as I shimmy and shake like I've lost my damn mind.

Every time Miley sings the lyric the song is named for, I switch it up and practically yell, "my best friend comes today" on beat with the music. I sing into my toothbrush, the cute pink one with extra soft bristles that Nico picked up after one too many times of me asking to borrow his, and sing into it before brushing my teeth.

I finish brushing my teeth and jump into Nico's arms, kissing him deep, our minty breaths mingling between us. He sets me down, laughing.

"Damn, baby girl; I know you're high energy, but this is next lexel."

I turn and shake my ass at him, earning a little love tap to my butt. I yelp in response. "Baby girl? Hmm...I kinda like it. Gives me some *Criminal Minds* vibes."

"Better than doll?"

I pop myself up onto the counter and think about his question, tossing my wild bedhead hair back and forth. "Honestly, Nico, you could probably call me shit head, and it would turn me on."

A thunderous laugh tears through his chest as he steps into me, giving me a long hug.

"I have to go to the office today, but I'll see you at dinner? I'm excited to meet your best friend."

I press my lips to his, kissing him between each word of my response.

"Yes."

Kiss.

"You."

Kiss.

"Will."

Kiss.

He groans as he pulls away. "I need to leave before I take you back to the bedroom and have my way with you."

"Better leave fast, then. I'm about to get naked and run soap all over my body."

Shaking his head with a small laugh, he turns and walks back into the bedroom.

After I finish getting ready for the day, I make the short drive to the Charlotte airport, waiting in the cell phone lot until my phone pings. I grasp it with excitement coursing through my veins.

Daphne: *The Bee-yotch has landed! See you in a few!*

Pulling to the curb outside the airport, I fling my door open, almost losing it to a car speeding in the lane next to me, and run to Daphne, wrapping her in the biggest hug imaginable. I love hugging Nico, love his strong arms and broad chest, but sometimes, you just need a hug from your main girl.

Daphne holds me at arm's length, cooing in her signature, raspy voice. "Girlfriend, you look good! Small town life looks amazing on you."

I help her hoist her bags into the surprisingly roomy trunk of my Mustang, and we climb into the car next to each other, giggling the entire time. Together, we navigate out of the nightmare of the airport arrival gates and head towards Colin's house where we are meeting everyone for dinner. On the drive, we swap stories. She tells me about everything that has been happening at our shop in Portland, and I tell her about my work here. She puts my mind at ease when she tells me that Matt hasn't shown his face since the night he threatened to burn our business down, but I don't miss the fear in her voice when she recounts that night.

As we slowly cruise into Johnson Creek, Daphne squeals, channeling Janice from Friends with a loud and over-punctuated, "Oh. My. God." Her eyes dart from side to side, taking in Main Street. "Holy shit, Mina! This place is fucking idyllic. It's like it's out of a mother fucking picture book!"

I've always had a mouth on me. I'm certainly not afraid of using a few well-placed sentence enhancers, but my best friend is on a whole other level. The woman could legitimately make sailors blush. Man, was my mom going to have a field day with her.

We pass Dina's Diner, Broken Sparrow, and several other local shops before turning on to Bougainvillea Drive, and as we pull in front of Colin's house, Daphne lets out a low whistle.

I let us into the house, leaving Daphne's luggage in my car. We're going to stay at Nico's house, like I do almost every night, but my mom insisted we come for dinner first.

"Back here," a deep voice I immediately recognize as my brother's booms from the back of the house, breaking through the laughter from the girls.

Following the sounds, we walk towards the kitchen,

and I pause, my hand on Daphne's arm, before we meet up with my family on the deck off the kitchen. "Promise me something?"

Daphne rolls her eyes, already knowing what I'm going to say. But I say it anyway. "Just, don't go all man-eater on him. It's still really fresh."

Walking through the sliding door, we're greeted with the most mouthwatering smells wafting off the grill. In the yard, the girls are playing with Stella. My mom sits in a chair, a glass of wine at her side, while Colin stands beside the grill, tongs in hand.

My mom stands and gives Daphne a gentle hug as they exchange pleasantries. For as short as my mom is, Daphne is even shorter at an even five feet tall. We move over to Colin, and while my crazy best friend keeps it tame - by her standards - she still manages to swing her long black, hair over her shoulder, run a hand up his arm, and throw a wink as we move to say hi to the girls and Stella. As I'm finishing introductions, Nico comes into view, walking into the backyard from the side of the house.

"Holy fuck," Daphne hisses through clenched teeth as he walks towards us. We have taken up purchase on two lounge chairs, drinks in hand. "If every man in this town looks the way these two do, I'm never fucking leaving!"

I laugh as Nico comes to stand next to me, reaches down to take my hand and pulls me to my feet. He wraps me in his arms, leaning his face down to mine to capture my lips in a quick kiss. Daphne makes an exaggerated gagging noise, gaining loud giggles from Emily and Laurel.

"Nico, meet my *wonderful*," I say with an eye roll, "best friend, Daphne."

He laughs and reaches out to shake her hand as she replies, "Oh, yes; I've been dying to meet you since the night Mina got back here and told me about her little vibrator incident on the plane!"

I lob a pillow from the lounge chair at Daphne, which she ducks to miss, not even spilling a drop of wine from the glass perched delicately in her hand. Nico lets out a thunderous laugh that encapsulates the entire back yard while my brother, mother, and nieces stare at me in utter horror.

The heat creeps up my neck, to my cheeks, and while in that very moment I wish for nothing more than a giant sinkhole to open beneath my feet. Knowing the likelihood of that happening is beyond slim to none, I do the second best thing and completely down my glass of wine before walking into the kitchen to refill my glass.

Sixteen

Nico

S ITTING around the table on a Friday night with Mina, her family, and her best friend has me feeling senti-mental for a time long ago when I would sit around the dinner table with my parents and sister. During the week, my sister and I were often at practice for one of the many sports teams we played for during our school years, but every Sunday, we sat around the table as a family.

The conversation easily flows around the table. Colin's two young girls excitedly talk about their soon-to-start school year while Daphne and Mina recount stories of their time together in Portland. Pauli tells us about an upcoming trip her women's auxiliary club is taking to Washington DC, and Colin talks about taking the girls on a vacation, asking them where they'd most like to travel. And me...well, I sit mostly quiet, enjoying the company around me while watching Mina interact with the people she loves the most.

I zone out and tune back in just in time to hear Daphne speak. "Hey, Mrs. P! Are you ever going to let Mina give you a tattoo?"

Mina almost snorts wine out her nostrils, quickly covering her mouth and nose with her dainty hand.

Pauli looks at Daphne, steel in her eyes, taking us all by surprise when she says, "Oh, sweet Daphne. My body is like a Mercedes, and you would never put a bumper sticker on a Mercedes, would you?"

This time, I'm fairly certain wine actually does come out of Mina's nose.

"How about you, Colin? When are you going to get some ink?" Daphne asks casually.

He shrugs noncommittally. "Already got one."

All five women at the table snap their heads to look at him in response, shrieking. A chorus of "what" and "you do not" drifts from every corner of the table we're seated around.

Part of my duty as a best friend is to know almost everything about Colin, so this little piece of news doesn't come as a surprise to me. His mother, daughters, and sister, however, look at him like he has sprouted a second head. Daphne just stares at him, and I'm fairly certain I can see hearts growing in her eyes.

We talk for about another hour, Colin refusing to give up the location and design of his tattoo; spoiler alert: it's a rose on his hip that he got when he was 19. Slowly, we carry the remains of our meal into the kitchen, Pauli waving us all off when we offer to help with the cleanup. Mina grabs a few changes of clothes, most of them already at my house. Her and Daphne climb into the Mustang, me following closely behind in my truck.

When we get back to my house, Mina shows Daphne to a guest room before meeting me in my room. No, not my room- our room. Because despite the fact that she doesn't live here yet, she will one day.

"Thank you for letting Daphne stay here," she says quietly, coming up behind me and wrapping her arms around me. "It means a lot to me."

I turn, still within the circle of her arms, and press my lips to hers. She melts into me, my arms going around her, and my God, do I love it. It takes all the strength I have not to carry her to our bed and slide into her, but I know she is eager for time with her friend, so after kissing her lightly once more, I release her from my arms.

She quickly changes into a skimpy pair of terry cloth

shorts and surprises me when in lieu of her normal sleep tank, walks over to my dresser and slips one of my old tees over her head.

"Hope you don't mind." She shrugs, glancing towards me as I stand, mouth agape, in awe of how sexy she is.

Groaning in response, I walk to her, giving her ass a little squeeze as I whisper in her ear, "Next to nothing, I think this might be my favorite thing I've ever seen you in."

Giggling as she scurries out of the door, she turns before she gets to the guest room and blows me a kiss while giving me a wink.

I take a shower and walk downstairs in a pair of gray sweatpants - and only gray sweatpants - not expecting to find Mina and Daphne in the living room drinking wine in front of the wood burning fireplace.

"Yo, hottie," Daphne all but yells over the sounds of their music while waving a wine glass at me, "be a doll and take that fine ass into the kitchen to grab us a refill, please!"

Shaking my head, I walk to the kitchen to get their wine bottle, grabbing a beer for myself, before sitting down in a nearby chair.

Daphne, I'm learning quickly, has absolutely no filter. I don't mind, actually, I think it's hysterical. Also, the thought of what that woman would do to poor Colin makes me laugh just thinking about it.

"Here's to the first fire in the house," I say, tilting my beer in the direction of the fire.

Mina laughs; God, I love her laugh. "I'm sorry," she says, dragging out the word while slightly wine drunk. "We just thought it would be fun to break it in."

"Sorry if you planned on breaking it in for the first time with Mina naked in front of it on a bearskin rug, Nico," Daphne chimes in while arching her eyebrows.

I laugh, my hand coming up to gruffly rub across my chin, a telling grin on my face. "One, you're kinda crazy," I say, pointing at Daphne. "Two, don't think that thought hasn't crossed my mind at least once. And three," I point to Mina, holding eye contact with her, "you never have to apologize to me for anything."

I finish my beer, answering every question Daphne throws my way. Yes, I have a sibling. No, I've never owned a pet. Yes, I've been arrested. No, it wasn't for murder. Then, wanting to give the girls some time together, I give Mina a hug and quick kiss, tell Daphne goodnight, and make my way upstairs. Still buzzed on wine, Mina thinks she is whispering, but is doing the absolute opposite. While I've only just met Daphne today, I am fairly certain she has no volume other than loud, so while I'm not trying to eavesdrop on their conversation, I hear them talking as I take the last few steps to our bedroom.

"I love him for you, Mina. He is fucking dreamy. Like, did you *see* him in those fucking sweatpants?"

I laugh, secretly pleased with myself that I seem to have passed the best friend test. But then Mina talks, in an exaggerated whisper that she honestly thinks is quiet, and when she speaks, it takes my breath away.

"Daphne," she pauses for several long moments, "I think that I'm staying in Johnson Creek."

I freeze in the doorframe, any additional conversation from downstairs evaporating in the air. Mina is thinking of staying here. With me. I knew going into this that there was always the possibility of her returning to her life in Portland, to her business and her friends and whatever shitty men she kept stumbling upon. I always expected there to be an expiration date on the "us" we were building, and I knew it was going to be fucking horrendous when it happened. I knew she would take not just a piece of my heart but my entire fucking heart with her when she left. But now, she was really thinking of staying, and that was the only thing that mattered.

I crawl into bed and drift off to sleep as endless giggling and the aroma of the wood burning in the fireplace come wafting up through the house only to be awoken shortly after three in the morning. At first, I'm not sure what is happening as sleep disorients me, but I quickly wake up when I realize that Mina is between my legs, her lips tightly wrapped around my hardening cock.

"Fucking hell," I groan. "If this is a dream, don't ever wake me up."

She giggles around my dick, and the vibration makes my balls clench in anticipation of their impending release. Licking and sucking and biting, she's a greedy little girl. Her tongue traces from root to tip, deliberately spending extra time on each of the four barbells piercing my shaft. She palms my balls, tugging with just the right amount of pressure before she slides my dick from her mouth, where it bounces against my stomach and comes to rest covered in her spit.

Mina looks up at me, those unfathomably deep green eyes filled with lust and need and want. "Nico," she fervently gasps, "I want you to use me. I need you to use my mouth."

"Jesus Christ, Mina."

I've never moved so fast in my life, climbing off the bed, eagerly pushing off my pants the remainder of the way. I grab Mina and roughly pull her to me, taking her lips in a sloppy kiss and biting her lip until she whimpers. I ask her if she is sure that she wants this, and she responds with a simple nod. I push her to the mattress, speaking as I arrange her so she is laying with her head hanging over the side of the bed, looking at me upside down.

"Mina, I will use you." I trace her lips with my thumb. "I will use that pretty fucking pouty mouth of yours, but you need to tell me if it's too much. If you need me to stop, squeeze my leg twice, and I'll stop, no questions asked."

"I'm not going to ask you to stop, Nico. I'll only ever ask you for more."

This fucking woman, an evil little temptress, a magical siren singing the sweetest fucking song and luring me to her rocky shores all the while knowing I would gladly throw myself upon them over and over and over again if it meant I lived every day with her scent on my skin.

The high bed is the perfect height for her to be eye level with my cock. I step closer, and she immediately opens wide. Reaching out, I languidly trace both thumbs over the column of her neck as I slide my dick into her hot, wet mouth. She wants me to use her, and use her, I will. After two slow strokes, I sink my cock into her mouth until I'm pressing my balls against her face. Mina tenses under me, and I reassure her by gently caressing the side of her face.

"Relax, doll. Relax and breathe through your nose. You've got this."

She gives a small, upside down nod as I slide out and back in, quickly picking up speed. I can feel my cock slide down the back of her throat, feel her spit coating me and spilling over the side of her mouth, feel every little vibration from every little moan that comes from that deliciously dirty mouth. I slide two fingers into her mouth on either side of my dick, sliding back into her throat even further. She gags and gasps around my cock but doesn't spit me out. From underneath me, I can see beautiful tears streaking her face, running upwards towards her hairline before plummeting to the floor below us.

Her arms leave her sides, and for the slightest of moments, I think she is going to squeeze me, to tap out, but no. Instead she reaches behind me and grabs my ass, pulling me closer while she sucks in her cheeks and hollows them against me. My hands come to hold her face, one resting on either side, and I fuck her face. I fuck her face like I would die if I stopped. My hips buck against her as I feel my orgasm building in my balls.

I've gone caveman, grunting and groaning in appreciation of the mouth I worship with my dick, barely able to mutter aloud, "Mina, I'm going to come down your throat. You fucking take it for me, doll."

She moans against me, and with that, I come undone, stilling as my come spills down her throat. My beautiful girl takes it all, swallowing down what I give her, not spilling a drop, and when I finally pull from her mouth, the prettiest string of spit and cum trails from her lips to my dick.

Several minutes later, the starbursts behind my eyes subside and my breathing slows. Mina curls up around me as we both take our respective sides of the bed.

"What was that for?" I ask, still out of breath.

She looks shy, hesitant for a split second. "I'm," she stutters before continuing, "I'm not going back to Portland."

Without pause, a giant, goofy grin spreads across my face, my cheeks hurting from the strain of my smile. "Move in with me. Stay with me here, in this house. I won't sell it. This house, it can be ours."

Startled, she sits up, wide-eyed and lips parted. "You...you really want me here all the time?"

I pull her hand into mine and nod, sure she can hear just how loudly my heart is beating.

And then, she launches herself into my arms, toppling us over, Mina on top of me while emphatically nodding her head yes.

Seventeen

MINA

The world would be a better place if everyone was afforded a support system like I have. Thanks to Daphne, what little I still had in Portland would be arriving at Nico's house - our house - in a few days. My brother, my nieces, even my mom, seemed genuinely happy for me.

I only moved in a few weeks ago, but we settled nicely into a routine. We wake together in the mornings, eat dinner together on days I'm not working, and fall into bed each night in a mess of sheets and limbs. Even with the routine, days off when Nico isn't showing houses are quickly becoming my favorite. We spend those days in the study, a gorgeous room off the main entrance of the house. Nico had a massive window seat built under the large bay window, and with the natural lighting, it was the perfect place to get lost in my sketchbook while he worked at the oversized desk we found at a local antique store.

Today, though, I had a full day at Broken Sparrow, and as much as I wanted to stay cozied up with natural light pouring in on my face from my perch, I had to pull together an outfit and head towards the shop.

I settled on dark skinny jeans, a loose, lightweight black knit sweater, and knee-high black boots. The air had shifted recently, fall definitely upon us, and I was relishing the chance to wear cozy sweaters and chunky cardigans.

I come downstairs and walk behind Nico who is diligently working on something, wrapping my arms around his neck from behind. "Hey, I gotta run."

He swivels in his chair to face me before pushing himself to his feet. "Let me take you in today, and then, we can grab dinner on our way home."

Pressing my lips to his with a smile on my face, I respond. "I would love that."

I recently picked up two additional days each week at the shop with demand being higher than ever. It's a great feeling to be so well respected in my line of work that people actually travel to see me. But at the same time, it makes me miss Nico even more when we're apart. If nothing else, my increased work schedule has shown me just what an amazing caregiver he is. He often offers to interrupt his own workday to drive me to mine. He'll sometimes have dinner waiting for me when I get home at night. He's run me more than one fantastic bubble bath that usually ends with him in the tub with me. He's all rough and gruff on the exterior, but ooey gooey goodness on the inside.

I think back to the first time I locked eyes with him at the airport, how smug he looked. He still sometimes gives off that vibe when we're around people we don't know, but I've come to learn those are just the high walls he keeps up around everyone except the select few he trusts. I feel honored that I'm one of those few.

Nico parks the truck across the street from Broken Sparrow and ushers me towards the front door, hand firmly splayed on my lower back. As we walk, a few stray leaves crunch under my boots, and I take a minute to inhale deeply, the scent of fall wafting around us on the gentle breeze.

Always the gentleman when it comes to me, he holds the door open then follows me through as we walk to the appointment book behind the front desk. Raven greets us in her signature cheerful way, air kissing me on each cheek before tossing a sly wink in Nico's direction.

He laughs as I scan the book, my finger tracing down the four appointments I have for the day.

"See you around eight?"

I nod and give him a hug. When I pull away, he gently tilts my chin upward and places a closed mouth kiss on my lips. As he walks towards the door, he looks back at me. "You're amazing, doll. One of these days, you're going to do some work on me."

"Don't hold your breath," I yell as the door closes behind him.

I don't have a ton of rules when it comes to my clients. Of course, I won't touch someone underage unless their parent is with them and signs the necessary consent forms. Even then, I won't do the work if it is something that could potentially affect their life. Neck tattoos, hand tattoos, anything on the face - I was not doing that on anybody who wasn't well established in the world of body modification. I also didn't make a habit of tattooing men that I was dating. Sure, when I was in my early twenties, I may have inked a few guys I had gone on casual dates with, but now that I was older and established, I treated each piece I did like a sacred piece of art. It isn't that I couldn't do that for men I dated, I just didn't want to. I didn't want to spill my soul into something so intimate as my artwork only for us to break up at some point and for the man to end up resenting the piece. Or worse yet, to get the artwork removed. And that's exactly why I vehemently kept telling Nico I would not be on the giving end of his next tattoo.

I worked through my first two appointments of the day, a few nautical stars - how cliche - and a cute little butterfly that came from my rotating flash. The shop was abuzz with the sounds of machines humming, music playing in the background, and friendly chatter throughout the air. Just as I was finishing up necessary sanitation of my station, Thom stuck his head out from his office and asked me to come over.

"What's up?" I asked when I walked in and plopped into a seat across from his desk. Thom and I had become friendly over the last several months, and it wasn't uncommon for him to pull me into the office to bounce ideas back and forth.

"I think it's almost time," he said. When I look at him quizzically, he sighs and continues, "I'm ready to cut back my hours here. The shop is in a great place; we have a higher demand than we can even keep up with. You've done a great deal for us, and I'd like to extend an offer to you to come on full time in a slightly different capacity than you're currently in."

My eyes go wide. "You're retiring?"

"Not fully, but I would like to begin to show you

more of the behind the scenes. Ordering, profit and losses, employment contracts..." he trails off as he looks to me. "This place has been in my family for generations; you know that. My son is young, too young to want anything to do with Broken Sparrow, and if I am going to leave it in the hands of someone, I want that person to be respected and trusted by their peers. You've shown that in the short time you've been here. Hell, even Raven likes you. And don't let her fool you, she may appear sweet, but she hates almost everyone."

I laugh, tears filling my eyes in gratitude as I look to Thom. "I would love nothing more than to help you in any way I can."

He stands, coming around the desk, and takes me in a rare hug. Not a sensual or passionate hug, but a hug that conveys how much this means to him, to his family.

He nods towards the office door, "We can get started next week, talk with Raven and carve out a few hours each day."

The rest of my day flies by as I tackle a larger floral piece on a petite woman's bicep. Four hours into intricate outlines, we end the first appointment and set up a follow up to complete the color.

Two other artists are working alongside me tonight, and I decide to spend some time with Raven, learning the customer database system the shop uses. It's old and rudimentary and I immediately add new customer management software to my mental list of small changes to implement at the shop.

John and Willow, the two other tattoo artists who are working tonight, finish up and head out, leaving just Raven and myself behind. We chat as we leisurely stock a few shelves with Broken Sparrow merchandise: keychains, t-shirts, and hats- all locally sourced. She tells me about her flavor of the week, a girl named Wren. I laugh, telling her it sounds an awful lot like fate, Raven and Wren, two birds of a feather.

We finish cleaning the shop, disinfecting all surfaces thoroughly, taking out the trash, cleaning the bathroom; the menial tasks most people scoff at. I have about fifteen minutes to kill before Nico comes to pick me up, but there isn't much else to do, so I tell Raven to head out for the night.

"Thanks for always being so nice to me," she says with a wave as she leaves through the front door.

I like Raven; I actually like her a lot. I get the feeling that people haven't always been kind to her, and a part of me understands that more than she knows. It's hard enough to be young; it's even harder to live an alternative lifestyle than what the masses consider "normal." Tattoos, piercings, crazy hair colors; it has all become somewhat more acceptable within society, but many people still scoff, assuming us to be less educated or less likely to hold down good paying jobs. Little do those close minded fuckers know, I make absolute bank.

Alone in the shop, I turn off the rock that had been coursing through the place and instead tune into the gentle sounds of Ray LaMontagne. I sway to his music as I chase a broom around the space, softly singing to myself, my mind drifting to the sexy man who will be coming for me any minute.

I hear the small bell chime over the door and call out without looking, "Hey, sexy man; I've been waiting for you!"

When he doesn't respond, I turn to look towards the door only to find that it isn't Nico at the door.

It's Matt.

And he looks pissed.

I freeze in place, broom still in hand, my eyes tracking him as he leans back against the door and locks it before moving to the neon open sign, flicking it off. The sound of the lock turning sends shivers down the length of my spine.

My eyes flick to the clock above the front desk- 7:55 PM- before falling back on Matt. Five minutes. I can make it five minutes.

He advances on me, and I shove the broom between us, but he tosses it aside, grabbing my wrist harshly with his hand. He has scared me before, but nothing like this. Right now, I'm fucking terrified.

Matt twists my arm behind my back, pressing me into the nearest table normally used for tattooing clients. I whimper, but refuse to beg him to let me go knowing he never will. He pins me to the table with his hips to my body, a hand pressing my face into the material covering it, and I'm disgusted when I realize he is hard against me.

He seethes as he speaks, and I can feel the heat radiating off his body and his words. "I told you I wasn't fucking done with you. You ran from me, and I don't let things I want get away from me."

He pulls me flush with his body, one hand greedily pushing up my shirt as the other grasps tight around my neck. I feel tears prick at my eyes as he fumbles with my bra, pulling it down to expose my breasts. His hand cups my breast as his grip tightens around my throat, causing me to gasp for breath.

Pushing me back to the table, my bare chest on the cold, vinyl fabric, I hear the teeth of his zipper. He presses his face into the crook of my neck, inhaling me. "I've missed the way you smell, sweet girl."

This time, I can't help myself. "Stop," I plead.

"I don't think I will," he responds dryly.

Tears stream down my face as I openly sob beneath

him, waiting for him to have his way with me in a place that has always felt sacred to me. My church, my sanctuary. And he wants to take that from me just like he took so much else from me already.

My eyes fly open as his hands come to sit on the waistband of my denim clad legs, reaching around to unfasten the button. I scan the shop for something, anything I can use against him to stop this from happening, but nothing is within my reach.

Feeling defeated, I go to squeeze my eyes shut again, willing myself to make it through this unscathed physically. I already feel the mental anguish taking root deep within. I glance at the clock once more- 8:02 PM.

And then, before I can shut my eyes, the sound of a large crash ricochets through the shop, glass shattering inward and into the studio, causing Matt to jump back from me, his pathetic half hard dick swinging between his legs as he turns towards the sound.

Eighteen

Nico

Mina texted me this afternoon to tell me that she had news- huge news- but that she didn't want to tell me over the phone. I've been thinking about it all day, wondering what she has to tell me. I am running a few minutes late to pick her up and have tried to call her three times, but her phone keeps ringing to voicemail. Something doesn't sit right in my stomach; she usually picks up.

I pull in front of the studio, throwing my truck into park, and glance to see the light indicating the shop is open has already been switched off. Most lights had been turned off, but I could still see faint shadows bouncing off the walls.

I climb out of the truck, straining to see through the

window. Vomit rises in the back of my throat when my mind catches up with what my eyes are seeing.

Mina- my beautiful Mina- is pressed against a table, her breasts exposed, and tears are streaming from her eyes as some monster of a man presses himself up behind her.

I try the door, only to find it locked. At once, every fiber of my being vibrates with anger and I am desperate to get to Mina, to stop the pain and hurt being inflicted on her.

Looking around, I can't find anything strong enough to break the floor to ceiling glass pane windows that line the shop, but I don't let it deter me from reaching her. My body operates on autopilot, only aware of the need to reach Mina. Without thinking, I run back to the driver side door of my truck, engine roaring to life, and before I know what is happening, I slam the truck over the curb and into the front of the studio. Glass shatters around my truck as I reverse just enough to allow myself room to get out of the truck and climb through the now smashed window.

I stride towards the man, his half-flaccid dick hanging between his legs as he backs away from Mina.

"Call the cops," I bark, harsher than I want to speak to her, before charging the man. My hand connects with his jaw, his head jerking from the contact. I don't relent, my hand coming around his neck as I press his body against the wall. His feet come up off the ground as he gasps for air. My hand tightens further, spit trickling from the corner of his mouth.

"Nico, stop!"

Her desperate voice cuts through the air as she pleads with me, snapping me back to the present, and I quickly release my hand from this man's throat, sending him to the ground in a heap, gasping for breath.

I take one more look at the man, then make quick moves to reach Mina. She is still near the table, her phone clutched in her hand. She reaches for me, and when I pull her into me, she collapses, a cacophony of gut wrenching sobs tearing from her throat as full body convulsions course over her.

"I...I was so scared."

I gently stroke her hair, keeping one eye on the stranger across the room, shushing her and whispering words of reassurance in her ear as approaching police sirens wail in the night.

I call Thom and tell him what happened at the shop, promising to pay for the damage to the building while Mina speaks with two officers. The man, that I've since learned is Mina's disgusting ex-boyfriend Matt, is cuffed and placed in the back of a police cruiser. The officers were nice enough to allow him to pull his pants all the way up before escorting him from the building. I wouldn't have afforded him the same respect, preferring to embarrass him even further by leaving his humorously small cock on display for the onlookers gathering outside the shop.

Thom arrives a few minutes later. "Jesus Christ."

"I didn't know what else to do," I offer weakly.

He places a hand on my shoulder. "I'm not mad. I'm just happy she is safe."

Shortly after, Colin and Pauli arrive and rush to Mina. She is incredibly brave as she tells the story over and over again. First to the cops, then to Thom, and finally to her family. Exhaustion clouds her normally cheery features and through the entire night, she holds onto my hand tightly although a void fills her gaze.

Thom runs to a 24-hour store to grab a few tarps, and when he returns, I help him cover the smashed windows the best we can. He leaves, wanting to give Mina time with her family, but before he does, he shakes my hand- a firm handshake- and tells me again how not only is he not angry at me, but he is thankful that I was there to keep Mina safe, no matter the cost to the shop.

Mina and I will have to go to the station tomorrow to fill out more witness forms and to finish with questions, but tonight, she is rightfully overcome with exhaustion and emotion. She decides that she is going to press charges, and I'm proud of her for that, for taking control over some asshole that tried to take away her dignity.

Pauli comes up to me while Mina and Colin are talking and wraps me in an unexpected embrace. "Nicolas," she says with arms still around me, "thank you for taking care of my Philly." I nod, hugging her back as Colin and Mina rejoin us.

Colin mostly practices family law but vows to help Mina in any way possible, to make sure that Matt never steps foot near Mina again, that he can never hurt her again. Yes, he is family, and I know he would do anything for his sister, but I am still grateful that he is there to support her.

Colin and Pauli leave as Mina picks up a broom, sweeping up pieces of glass that were strewn around the room with the impact of my crash. I move to stop her, letting her know that Thom already said he'd be closing the shop tomorrow and would take care of it. I know she isn't fragile; she's shown me time and time again that she is anything but. However, I also know she is extremely vulnerable right now, and the thought of her sweeping up shards of glass caused by her attacker- her ex- churns my stomach.

She props the broom against the front desk, slowly running her fingers over the wood as she really looks around the shop. She walks to me, tears still streaking her cheeks.

Her frail voice comes out as a whisper, "Hold me, Nico."

I wrap my arms around her, and I hold her right there amongst the broken glass and tarps and table where I almost lost her.

She sobs against my chest. "I was so scared."

"Me, too, baby; me, too." I manage to mutter against her hair as I pull her even deeper into my arms, tears filling my own eyes.

Her cries leave her body in small whimpers. "I didn't know what he was going to do. I knew it was going to be bad, but all I kept thinking was 'what if he loses all control? What if I never get to see you again?'"

My hand lightly rubs circles on her back as I repeat those words to her that I first spoke in that small bed at her brother's house all those weeks ago.

"You're safe with me, sweetheart."

I kiss the top of her head.

"I won't let anything happen to you, Mina."

I kiss her temple.

"You are so fucking strong, baby."

I kiss her cheek.

"You are so incredibly brave and beautiful, Mina."

I ever so gently kiss her lips.

Her eyes don't meet mine, and I'm terrified that this is the beginning of her shutting me out. I am scared shitless that this asshole has succeeded in taking her from me despite not physically being in her life. I reach to my own eyes, swiping a few of my own tears with the pad of my thumb.

But this is Mina. And even when she is dealing with her own demons, her own grief, she cares fiercely for those around her at the same time. Finally, her eyes raise to meet mine, and when she notices my tears, she pushes up to kiss them away with her perfect lips before repeating almost the same words I said to her just minutes earlier.

"I'm safe with you, Nico."

She kisses me.

"I won't let anything happen to us."

She kisses me again.

"You are so fucking strong."

Another kiss.

"You are so incredibly brave and beautiful, Nico."

Another kiss.

I pull her back to my lips, kissing her again. "I thought those were my lines, baby?"

And through her pain and extreme anguish, she does the most Mina-like thing ever. She giggles.

Fuck, I am so utterly gone when it comes to this

creature standing in front of me. She's summer rain and autumn leaves, waves crashing against the coast and glasslike still waters. She's pain, and pleasure, and spicy, and sweet- so fucking sweet- all rolled into the most perfect fucking package ever. And somehow, I am the lucky bastard that gets to call her mine. I'll never be good enough for her, but fuck, I'll spend every day of my life showing her just how worshiped she is.

She walks to the small break room in the back of the shop, coming back with her purse. Her hand stretches out to mine, and I lace my fingers with hers, holding her tight, afraid to let her go, afraid if I let her out of my sight for even a nanosecond that something or someone will tear her from me. And again, seeming to sense that I need reassurance from her as much as she needs it from me, she looks at me, her gaze dropping to our hands, and she simply whispers, "take me home, Nico. Please take me home."

Nineteen

MINA

I HAVE NEVER BEEN as scared in my entire life as I was tonight. Every time I blink, I'm assaulted with flashes of Matt. The rage in his eyes chilled me to my core, and when he advanced on me, I tried desperately to find enough fight to push him away, but I froze. The entire time he was behind me, baring me and touching me, all I could think about was Nico. I pictured him in my mind: his attentiveness, his compassion, his love. I was afraid he would find me damaged after I was marked by this man who once claimed to care for me, afraid he wouldn't want me anymore- so damn afraid.

We reach his now dented truck, Nico helping me into the cab before circling to the driver's side. He lifts the center console, pushing it into the seat back before pulling me across the cab. I settle close to him, his arm securely around me the entire drive home.

Walking into the house, the silence is almost deafening.

I inhale and smell Matt on my skin. Retching, I run to the small half bath on the first floor, the lack of food from the day causing nothing but bile to expel itself from my stomach. Nico is quickly at my side, pulling tendrils back from my forehead with one hand as he rubs my back with the other. "I..." I choke out between heaves, "I need his smell off of me. I can't- Nico, I can't take it."

He pulls my limp body from the cool tile of the floor, scooping me into his arms. His touch is tentative and tender. I feel safe with him, and I instinctively reach up, wrapping my arms around his neck. He walks with purpose to the stairs, the long strides of his shoe clad feet echoing in the still quiet house. We reach the steps, but I stop him before he can begin to climb them. "I can walk."

"I know you can. I know there isn't anything you can't do on your own, but I need this right now, Mina. I need to know that you are mine, and so help me God, if that means carrying you upstairs and washing his scent off of you, so fucking be it."

I go to speak, but he cuts me off, not putting me

down. "I was so fucking afraid I was going to lose you, Mina. I was petrified when I looked in that window and saw him touching you, when I saw the tears coming down your face. You were so close, but I couldn't get to you. I needed to get to you!"

I press my fingers to his lips. "Hey, hey, hey..." I speak fast, "You *did* get to me. You stopped it. You stopped him, and you saved me, Nico. Without you, I don't know what would have happened. I don't even want to think about it. But I'm safe. I'm safe, and I'm yours, and I'm not going anywhere, love."

He finally exhales, and I can tell he has been holding that breath for what probably seemed like an eternity. As broken as I feel inside, he feels it, too. He shares in my pain, and in this moment, I share in his. I slide my shaking hand to his cheek. "I'm okay. *We're* okay." Then, I nod my head towards the stairs, and he climbs them, holding me as if I'm both weightless and the most precious cargo he has ever held in his arms.

We enter the bathroom, and he sets me down in front of the sink. I clumsily reach for my toothbrush, knocking over a few bottles as my hands continue to tremble. Nico comes behind me, reaches for the tube of extra whitening toothpaste on the counter, and squeezes the tube until a glob falls onto my brush. I thrust the brush into my mouth, scrubbing away the taste of bile that coats my mouth. Nico moves to our bath, turning the water on, and as the water rises, I can see the steam wafting from the tub. He adds a healthy amount of bubbles and comes back to me, stilling with his chest to my back. He's so broad and strong against me, a pillar of strength in an ancient, crumbling city, a lighthouse signaling to lost souls at sea.

I'm the lost soul, and he found me on that plane from Portland. I just didn't know how lost I was at the time. He captured me with his light, guiding me to him and making me whole by offering me a piece of his heart.

He reaches around me, taking a brush from the counter. Ever so gently, he removes the elastic that has been holding my hair, letting the tangled tresses fall around my face and shoulders. Brush in hand, he runs it through my tangles in one of the most intimate experiences of my life. But then again, I feel like my entire existence with Nico has centered around small, intimate experiences that show me just how much he truly cares. It's in his stolen glances and kisses. In the ease at which he invited me into his home- our home- in surprise pieces of pie and shared showers. It's in every gentle touch and every whisper against my ear when he thinks I've fallen asleep. And though I'm scared at how quickly our relationship has progressed, equally as terrified with what happened tonight, in this moment, with this broad-chested man behind me, I know without a doubt that he is my home, and I want nothing more than to spend my entire life with him by my side.

His voice is raspy, barely a whisper as he speaks. "Come on, my sweet doll. Let's get you in the tub."

I allow him to undress me, too exhausted to muster the strength to do it on my own. My gentle man looks to me for reassurance with each step, gauging my emotions. He peels my jeans and panties down my thighs, letting them pool at my feet before he urges my arms up over my head to gain access to my sweater. Lastly, he unclasps my bra, and I allow it to fall to the ground with the rest of my soiled clothes.

I cross to the tub, Nico close behind. As I stand beside the oversized bath, he extends his hand to me, steadying me as I climb in and melt into the hot water. He fills the room with gentle music and lights the few candles we have around the bathroom. I expect him to undress and slide into the tub next to me, but perhaps he senses my hesitation. Instead, he kneels down next to me, swiping his thumbs across my cheek.

"I'm going to give you some time alone." I nod as he continues, "It's late, and you need to eat something, doll, even if you don't feel like it. I'm going downstairs, and

I'm ordering us a pizza, I'll come get you when it arrives."

He walks to the pile of clothes on the floor and collects them under his arm. "I'm taking these and getting rid of them. I'll buy you a new outfit tomorrow. Hell, Mina, I'll buy you a whole new fucking wardrobe tomorrow if it makes you happy."

This earns a small laugh from me and I find the sides of my mouth curve up into a smile, the first one I've had in hours.

Leaving the room, I call after him, "Nico!"

He sticks his head back into the bathroom, looking at me through the glass of the oversize shower the tub sits within. All I can do is smile at him- a genuine smile with no hidden pretense.

He smiles back, a big goofy grin. "I love you, too, Mina."

Then, he is gone, and I can only hear his faint footsteps over the sound of the music wafting around the room as freely as the steam from the bath water that surrounds me.

I soak for what feels like hours, letting scalding water cleanse my skin. I wash my hair twice and scrub my body thoroughly. I top off the water, making it hotter as it cools, and pay no attention as some splashes over the edge into the enclosed shower around me.

The doorbell rings, echoing throughout the house, but I stay soaking, knowing Nico would take care of it just like he said he would. He is a man of his word, always making me feel beautiful and protected. It's just one of the many things I have come to love and admire about him.

A short time later, he appears in the doorway, having traded his jeans and button up for sweatpants and an old white tee. It's one of my favorite looks on him. He really is magnificent to look at in anything he wears, but when he wears a thin tee and I can see his tattoos outlined under the fabric, it just makes me swoon.

He helps me from the tub, pulling a fresh towel from the towel warmer and wrapping me tightly in it before handing me a second for my hair. I finish drying myself, run a comb through my hair, and tie it in a loose elastic on top of my head.

"Come down when you get dressed?"

I let the towel drop around me, unphased by Nico's gaze that looks longingly yet tentatively over my body. I wrap my arms around him, my bare body pressed against his clothed form, needing to feel his touch. His arms slide around me, and I push to my toes, landing a quick kiss on his lips. "I'm only coming down if I can wear one of your shirts."

"You can wear anything you want, baby."

He leaves me to change, and I pick a faded old Johnny Cash tee. Even with my height, it dwarfs me, hanging off my shoulder and almost down to my knees. I slide my feet into some slippers and pad my way towards the stairs.

I'm surprised when I glance to the bottom of the stairs and find Nico waiting. I'm two steps from the bottom when he lifts me off the stairs. Instinctively, my legs wrap around him, although I know he'll never let me fall.

He peppers featherlight kisses over my lips before he sets me down, sliding his hand into mine. He walks me through the house, playfully popping his hip into mine. "You look much better in that shirt than I ever have."

"That's hard to believe," I reply.

I expect to go into the kitchen and am surprised when he instead pulls me towards the living room. A fire is roaring to life in the fireplace, there is a blanket spread across the floor in front of it, and there is food, so much food that it is borderline gluttonous. Yes, there is pizza, but there is also pasta, fresh fruit and vegetables, bread with various dipping sauces, antipasta, and of course, peanut butter pie.

"You have to eat, even if you don't want to. I didn't know what you would want, so I got it all"

Laughter pours out from me. "I'd say so."

We sit on the ground together, music playing in the background. I nibble on some veggies while Nico inhales fresh mozzarella. He snags a cherry tomato from the oversized vegetable tray and playfully tosses it towards my face. Slightly off, it pings off my cheek and rolls across the floor. We both roar with laughter before I pick one up and toss it towards him, cheering when I sink the tomato right in his mouth.

"Nothing but net!"

Along with my time soaking in the tub, the laughter helps to ease some of the pain from the night, and I suddenly realize that I actually am hungry- starving, even. I stuff myself full of pizza, while of course, leaving room for pie.

We finish eating and move to the couch, basking in the low glow of the fire and each other's company.

"Do you want to talk about it?"

I'm not expecting the question. "Honestly, no."

He squeezes my hand as Ben Rector fills the room, pouring from the surround sound system Nico insisted on splurging for in the living room. Standing, his hand extends to mine. "Dance with me, Mina?"

I'm in his arms without hesitation, our bodies clumsily swaying together in time with the music, our own private dance, just for the two of us. He quietly sings along to the song, and just like everything else about him, his singing voice is so uniquely male. It is slightly raspy yet smooth, deep yet gentle.

Instantly, I am overcome with emotion, my breath hitching as silent tears trickle down my cheeks. He holds me tighter, stroking my hair.

"I'm going to marry you one day," he whispers in my ear as the song ends and fades into something new. "I'm going to marry you, and have children with you, and a dog with you, and maybe even a fucking cat with you. We're going to build a family together, Mina. We're going to grow old together sitting on the front porch of this house, and when you're an old lady with gray hair and faded tattoos, I'm going to love and worship you then just as much as I do now, baby."

Christ, I love this man. I love this man because he means every word he just said to me; he always does. He's my protector and my lover. He pushes my buttons at the same time as pushing me to be my best. I feel safest in his arms and always miss them when they are not wrapped around me.

And though I don't know what his definition of 'one day' means, I do know one thing for sure. When that day does come, I will absolutely say yes.

Epilogue

Nico

Six Months Later

I'm standing in Colin's office, him sitting behind his desk while I pace back and forth across the small room. My stomach is in knots, and I'm fairly certain I'm going to vomit all over the antique rug that sits under Colin's desk.

"You're sure she's going to say yes?" I ask, my words coming out hurriedly.

Colin laughs before standing and walking out from behind his desk. Clasping a palm over my shoulder, he nods his head. "I don't think I've ever been so sure about something in my life. You guys are definitely made for one another."

I smile, but his words do little to calm the anxiety coursing through my body.

Tonight, I'm going to ask Mina to be mine- forever.

As wild and untamed as Mina is, my total free spirit, she also values tradition. So, when I decided that I was going to ask Mina to marry me, I asked both Pauli and Colin for her hand.

"I'm going to fuck it up, Colin. I just know I'm going to make an ass out of myself. Let me practice with you?"

"Dude, what? No!"

I don't listen to Colin. Instead, I sink to one knee on his dingy, antique office carpet while producing a small velvet box from my pocket. Holding it out to him, I'm about to open the box when his door flies open.

Daphne stands in the doorway, mouth agape before absolutely losing herself in a fit of laughter. "Uh...do you guys need me to give you a sec?"

Colin pushes me backwards as he walks back to his chair. I'm able to right myself just before I lose my balance, and I quickly stand to my feet.

Daphne comes over to me, throwing herself at me in a huge hug. "I'm so fucking happy for you, Nico!" Looking back at Colin, she drops her voice. "And how are *you*, good looking?"

Turning back to me, Daphne squeals, "But for real, show me the goods!"

I hand her the box, and she flips the lid open. "Holy fuck, dude!"

She stares at the engagement ring I spent weeks picking. It's a delicate double halo ring, terminology I never would have expected I'd know in a million years. Almost three carats and completely vintage, it is the embodiment of Mina in diamond form.

I take the box back from Daphne, sliding it back into my pocket. "Okay, so everything is set. I'm headed to pick up Mina; I'll see you guys soon."

I close the office door behind me as I leave, but not before I hear Daphne say, "Okay, Colin, just you and me now. Whatever shall we do about that?"

Poor girl; she's got it bad.

Colin has admitted to me that he thinks Daphne is attractive; he just doesn't think he is ready to start dating again - especially something long distance. But if I'm being honest, I think they would be great together. Maybe she could get him to loosen up a bit, maybe even get rid of those monogrammed business shirts he insists on wearing.

I promised Mina we'd go out to dinner tonight, praying that she doesn't know what I'm up to. Picking her up at Broken Sparrow, we walk to the same Italian restaurant we ate at with Colin and his girls all those months ago. We share a bottle of wine and garlic knots -

extra Alfredo sauce please. She laughs when I recount the memory of her so sexily licking the sauce off her lips the first time we were here together, and she confides that she was overly flustered when I started stroking her bare thigh under the table.

We finish our meals, and before leaving, I excuse myself to the restroom, confirming with Colin that everything is set. Then, Mina and I slowly walk towards Broken Sparrow. We're almost to the truck when I pause. Mina takes a few steps before realizing I've stilled.

"Everything okay, love?"

"Um, yeah. I left my phone in the shop earlier. Can we grab it quickly?"

The shop, with its fantastic new windows, if I do say so myself, has been closed to customers for a few hours. I worked closely with Thom and Raven to set this up, and I couldn't have thought of a better way to do this than what we came up with.

Mina unlocks the front door, and I hold it open for her to enter in front of me. "Where do you think you left it?"

"Over by your station, I think."

She takes a few more steps, finally looking up, and stops in her tracks as her eyes go wide. The entire inside of the shop has been transformed, lowly lit with hundreds of candles in all colors of the rainbow. Fairy lights are strung across the ceiling, furniture has been pushed out of the way, and Leon Bridges quietly fills the space.

"Ni...Nico," she stutters, "what...what's going on?"

I take her by the hand and lead her to the center of the room, taking a few seconds to just look at her beautiful features. Knowing these are the last minutes she will possibly be just my girlfriend feels surreal.

"Mina," I start, "as cliche as it sounds, there is a part of me that thinks I fell in love with you the first second I saw you at the airport. And if that was love at first sight, you still find a way to make me fall deeper in love with you each and every day."

I brush a few strands of hair behind her ear, cupping her cheek before I continue. "You make my life more colorful, not only with your bright tattoos and hair, but with the simple act of just being you."

Leaning forward, I place a soft kiss on her lips. "I know that this shop holds one of the scariest days of your life - of my life, too. But I also know that it has become one of your favorite places, and I want it to also represent one of the best days of your life."

I drop to one knee while slipping the small box from my pocket. She utters a small gasp, eyes darting back and forth between my own.

"Would you do me the honor of being my wife, of allowing me to spend every day of the rest of my life loving and worshiping you, of allowing me to protect you and care for you? Will you grow old with me and have children with me? Will you have faded tattoos with me, and go on hikes with me, and eat pie with me for the rest of our lives? Simply put, Mina, will you marry me?"

She sinks to her knees, tears in her eyes. Hell, there are tears in my eyes, too. She cups my face in her dainty hands, her head bobbing. "Yes, Nico! Oh, my Gods, yes!"

I remove the ring from the box and slide it onto her finger. She looks at the ring and then launches herself at me. I catch her in my arms, still kneeling on the ground, as her lips crash over mine.

"Oh, Nico, I love you. I love you so much, and I think I fell in love with you on that first day, too. Even if I didn't want to admit it, it has always been you that I was waiting to find. Or maybe, I was waiting for you to find me."

I pull us to our feet, kissing her the entire time. The door to the break room opens, family and friends pouring out into the shop. Daphne walks up to us and hands us each a champagne flute. Mina does a double take before squealing in excitement. "Oh my God! You *knew*! You knew, and you kept it a secret!"

"Guilty as charged," Daphne calls out.

More champagne is passed around, and we all feast on Dina's Diner pie in celebration. Mina laughs. "Now I know why you wouldn't let me order dessert at dinner!"

I wink at her in response.

Soon after we've been congratulated by everyone, Raven pushes us out of the shop. "I've got everything taken care of. Go! Be newly engaged!"

Mina laughs, pulling her into a hug. She grabs my hand as we exit the shop and make our way to my truck. Before opening the door for her, I pull her against me once again, uttering the words that have become a mantra between us.

"You're safe with me, Mina."

I kiss the top of her head.

"I won't let anything happen to you, baby."

I kiss her temple.

"You are so amazingly strong, sweetheart."

I kiss her cheek.

"You are so incredibly brave and beautiful, doll."

I ever so gently kiss her lips.

And this time, I add one more line to our affirmations.

"I cannot wait to marry you, Mina."

THE END

Like Mina, women experiencing Domestic Violence are not weak. If you or someone you know is experiencing physical or mental abuse, seek help. The world needs your beauty and you are worth so much more.

National Domestic Violence Hotline

800-799-7233
or text START to 88788

Crisis Text Line

Text HOME to 741741

National Sexual Assult Hotline

800-656-HOPE

Acknowledgments

"It takes a village" isn't only true when it comes to raising children, but also when publishing a novel. When I first started to write Mina and Nico's story, I poured countless hours into it along with a piece of my soul. Along the way, I was blessed to find an amazing team of individuals, all of whom poured their time into this story as well.

First and foremost, an enormous thank you to Tiffany Thomas from Tiff Writes Romance for working with me as a first time author. You were instrumental in bringing this manuscript to life, helped to calm my nerves from our first conversation, and brought polish to my work with your incomparable editing.

To Tori Ellis at Cruel Ink Editing + Design, how

incredibly lucky am I to work with someone I admire immensely for my very first book. Your attention to detail and eye for design catapulted my ideas into reality and turned the layout for Inked into a work of art. From the bottom of my heart, thank you for answering the million questions I lobbed at you, for squeezing me into your already jam-packed schedule, and for walking me through the entire formatting process.

My amazing fiance, Laura, words cannot express my gratitude for your involvement in this project. From encouraging me to actually pursue my dream of writing, to reading my manuscript at least 1,000 times, to pushing me to share my work with the world. You have been there for me every step of the way, even when I am being needy and annoying, and for that, I am forever grateful. I can't wait to see what adventures we stumble upon next!

And of course, to every single one of you holding a copy of Inked in your hands. Thank you for reading Mina and Nico's story and for allowing me to create these small escapes from reality with my words. I truly love you all!

About The Author

Amity Malcom was born in Pennsylvania. She began writing short stories while still in elementary school including a total page turner about how her mother loved to fish. Her mother does not love to fish and is actually terrified by ocean creatures.

She now resides in Florida with her fiance, three completely insane but loveable cats and one neurotic but adorable dog.

When not writing steamy characters and happily ever afters, Amity can be found watching professional soccer, exploring Florida's many theme parks, and campaigning for LGBTQIA+ rights.

www.ingramcontent.com/pod-product-compliance
Lightning Source LLC
Chambersburg PA
CBHW060315310726
48976CB00007B/2331